Praise for

THE BOY AT THE END OF THE WORLD

A Bank Street Best Children's Book of the Year

"Both moving and full of adventure. This remarkable survival story will change the way readers think about themselves and the world they live in." —Sarah Prineas, author of *The Magic Thief*

"Part speculative fiction, part cinematic survival adventure, the novel features a brisk pace and clever and snappy dialogue." —*Kirkus Reviews*

"[A] quirky, high-stakes adventure. . . . A pleaser for readers who prefer their [science fiction] livened up with unpredictable elements and emotional complexity." —*Booklist*

"Fantastically clever and memorably creepy." —*BCCB*

"With strong themes of courage and self-reliance, this challenging and thought-provoking adventure is a fine choice for [a] science-fiction collection." —*SLJ*

"The characters are well developed and the moral dilemmas are sound. This is an excellent beginning for science fiction readers and the study of dystopian society." —*Library Media Connection*

"A boldly imagined future . . . exciting." —*Horn Book*

BOOKS BY GREG VAN EEKHOUT

. . .

Kid vs. Squid

The Boy at the End of the World

THE BOY AT THE END OF THE WORLD

Greg van Eekhout

NEW YORK LONDON NEW DELHI SYDNEY

First published in the United States of America in June 2011
by Bloomsbury Books for Young Readers
Paperback edition published in October 2012
www.bloomsbury.com

For information about permission to reproduce selections from this book, write to Permissions, Bloomsbury BFYR, 1385 Broadway, New York, New York 10018

The Library of Congress has cataloged the hardcover edition as follows:
Van Eekhout, Greg.
The boy at the end of the world / by Greg van Eekhout. — 1st U.S. ed.
p. cm.
Summary: Born half-grown in a world that is being destroyed, Fisher has instinctive knowledge of many things, including that he must avoid the robot that knows his name.
ISBN 978-1-59990-524-2 (hardcover)
[1. Science fiction. 2. Survival—Fiction. 3. Robots—Fiction.] I. Title.
PZ7.V2744Boy 2011 [Fic]—dc22 2010035741

ISBN 978-1-59990-918-9 (paperback)

Book design by Nicole Gastonguay
Typeset by Westchester Book Composition
Printed and bound in the U.S.A. by Thomson-Shore Inc., Dexter, Michigan
4 6 8 10 9 7 5

To Mike and Todd
(companions on early misadventures)

THE BOY AT THE END OF THE WORLD

CHAPTER 1

This is what he knew:

His name was Fisher.

The world was dangerous.

He was alone.

And that was all.

Fisher became born in a pod filled with bubbling gel. A plastic umbilical cord snaked from his belly. When he opened his eyes, the first thing he saw through the clear lid of the pod was destruction. Slabs of concrete and twisted steel fell to the floor amid clouds of dust. Severed wires spit sparks into the air. The world was coming apart.

Something told Fisher to get up, get out, run away while he still could.

The word *instinct* came to mind.

He pushed against the pod lid and it came open with a

hiss. The gel stopped bubbling and drained away through holes at the bottom of the pod. Cold air struck Fisher's wet skin when he sat up. It was the first time he'd ever been cold, and he hated it.

He'd made a mistake. He never should have opened the lid. He never should have made himself become born. Maybe if he just lay back down and closed the lid the gel would return and he could go back to sleep and he'd be warm and everything would be all right.

A huge, explosive thud hammered Fisher's ears. The ground shook and the dim lights in the ceiling wavered and died. It was some kind of disaster. Or an attack. Fisher didn't know anything about attacks, except that they were dangerous and should be avoided.

Pipes clanged against the floor and more debris rained down. More sparks, more dust. Bitter air stung his nostrils. Fisher had never smelled this smell before. In fact, it was pretty much the first thing he'd ever smelled. He was only a few moments old, after all, and hadn't had time to smell much. Somehow, though, he knew the smell meant things were burning around him.

There was no choice now. He had to make himself all the way born and get out of whatever this place was before everything burned and crashed around him. He swung his legs over the side of the pod and set his bare feet down on the cold floor. He took a step, and then another, and that was as far as he got. The umbilical tugged him back. It was still attached to his belly. He would have to yank it out if he was going to become all the way born. But there was just no way he could do that. He knew this wasn't how things were supposed to be. His birth was supposed to be soft. He was supposed to be soothed and bathed in light. He wasn't supposed to be alone.

Another shuddering *whomp*, and Fisher's ears popped. It felt like something massive had struck the building. Debris clattered down. A big chunk of ceiling fell right in front of him, and Fisher discovered another thing he knew: profanity. Profanity was a collection of words that helped express strong feelings.

Fisher uttered a word from his profanity collection now.

It was the first word he ever spoke.

If the ceiling chunk had struck his head, Fisher would have been dead. Over and done with. He couldn't accept the idea of dying before he'd even become fully born, so he wrapped his fingers around his plastic umbilical and gave it a mighty yank. The cord came out, spraying milky fluid and a little bit of blood, and Fisher bawled because now he was completely born and he knew there'd be no going back.

But he didn't bawl standing still.

He bawled while running and shouting profanity.

. . .

Fisher found more pods lining the walls of vast, caved-in rooms. The pods contained all kinds of animals.

In one room, the pods held dogs. In another, pigs. In yet another, goats.

One room was full of pods the size of his hand, thousands of them, and inside were bees and worms and butterflies.

Another room held only four pods, each many times the size of Fisher's own. Inside were elephants, their eyes shut, their curving tusks tinted blue through the gel.

All the pods were broken. The lights were out. The gel didn't bubble. Many were cracked, their gel oozing to the ground. And many more were completely crushed by fallen debris.

Fisher knew what death was. He had become born knowing. Death was failure. All the creatures in these pods had failed to survive.

He came to one last chamber, stretching into the smoky distance, where the pods were smashed and buried. From a mound of rubble emerged a slender brown arm. A human arm.

Fisher silently approached it. He brushed pebbles and dust from the damp fingers and touched the wrist.

Cold and still.

Another failure.

A noise drew Fisher's attention away from the dead human. Down the corridor, through a haze of powdery light, a creature was bent over another pod. The creature was a little larger than Fisher and roughly shaped like him: two arms and two legs, a torso, an oval head. It was shaped like a human, but clearly not a human. A machine of some kind. The word *robot* came to Fisher's mind.

The pod had been knocked partway off its support platform, and the dead human inside dangled out of it. The robot was doing something with the dead human's umbilical cord.

Fisher's breath quickened with fear. He pressed his lips together to keep from making a noise and took a slow step back, then another. His heel struck a fallen pipe, and, losing his balance, he went down hard.

The human-but-not-human creature's head snapped around, turning its human-but-not-human face to Fisher.

It moved toward him.

"Fisher," it said. "I have found you."

Fisher ran. He scrambled over shattered puzzle pieces of concrete, through lung-choking smoke, through rooms where flames licked at pods of dead fish. He found a shaft of chalky light from above and began climbing up a steep slope of debris. Loose bits of concrete slid away beneath his hands and feet, and he struggled not to go sliding down with them.

Behind him, he could hear the screechy movements of

the robot creature that knew his name, but the sounds grew fainter the higher up he climbed. He kept going until, at last, he stumbled out into moonlight.

He took a moment to understand his surroundings. Robot creatures could kill him, but so could his environment. He knew this in the same way he knew his name and knew profanity and knew what kinds of animals lay dead in their pods.

He was on the summit of a mountain formed from colossal slabs of granite. There were no buildings in sight. Scant patches of trees smoldered and smoked. Soil and rocks tumbled from collapsing ledges. He couldn't tell exactly what had just happened here, but he had a strong sense that the place of his birth had just been attacked from above. How, or by what, he couldn't say.

And, actually, he didn't care.

Later, he might.

But now? He just wanted to get away.

He took off at a jog down the mountain, his eyes never straying for long from the star-freckled night sky. As he descended, the way grew thicker with trees and ferns. Things rustled in the dark. Tiny eyes glinted with pinprick light from the high tree boughs.

Hints of old structures in the woods revealed themselves. There were small piles of concrete bricks and crumbling sections of walls. Anything could be hiding among them.

The word *predator* came to Fisher's mind. Predators were animals that used weaker animals as food. The eyes in the dark might belong to predators. The robot down in the ruined birthing structure might be a predator. To deal with predators, Fisher would have to make sure he was always the strongest animal. He needed a weapon.

Keeping watch for approaching predators, he crept up to the remains of a building. There was just a mostly fallen wall, overgrown with ferns and vines. From a jagged concrete slab protruded a thin steel rod, sticking straight up. It flaked with rust.

Fisher planted his foot against the concrete and grasped the rod with both hands. He bent it back, and then forward, and then back again, and continued like that until the rod snapped. The end was a jagged point of sharp nastiness.

Fisher knew what a spear was. Now he had one.

How had he known what a spear was? How had he known how to fashion one? His hands appeared to know things he didn't quite know himself. For instance, they knew how to build a fire. Fisher could almost feel his fingers clutching tinder. Dry grass made good tinder. Or bark. Or leaves. Or tree resin. If he had tinder, then he'd need a way to ignite a fire. He could use flint sparks, or sunlight focused through a lens, or wood sticks and a small bow. Once the tinder was lit, he would need kindling to keep the fire going. There were plenty of branches around to use as kindling.

Fisher wished he could build a fire now. Sticky gel and clammy sweat coated his skin. It was bad to sweat in the cold. He discovered he knew the word *hypothermia*. But now was not the time or place for a fire. A fire might keep predators away, but it might also signal his presence to things. Things like the robot. Better to get more distance from his birthing place.

A twig snapped behind him. Fisher spun around.

"Fisher," the robot said. "I have been looking for you."

It reached for him with a soot-stained hand.

Fisher used profanity and thrust his spear into the robot's chest.

CHAPTER 2

The mechanical creature's face was a hideous mask. Two yellow globes bulged where eyes should have been. In place of a nose was a pair of vertical slits. Its mouth was an ear-to-ear chasm covered by fine wire mesh. Red wires poked from a small crack in its head. Maybe a rock had fallen on it during the attack. Fisher wished it had been a larger rock.

The mechanical man grabbed the spear with both hands and slowly withdrew it from his chest. The shaft was smeared with oil.

"Please be careful," said the machine, handing Fisher back his spear. His voice buzzed and hissed. "You nearly punctured my hydraulic pump."

"What do you want?" Fisher said, ready to make another spear thrust. This time he'd aim for the machine's cracked skull.

"I want to help you."

Not what Fisher expected. He figured the machine

wanted to kill him. Tear his head off. Eat his brains and guts as mechanical-man fuel.

"Help me do what?"

"My directives are to help Ark-preserved species survive so that they may reproduce and repopulate the Earth."

Fisher didn't know what most of those words meant, and definitely not in that order. He decided the safest thing to do was kill the mechanical man. Just as he prepared to spring, the machine's head swiveled around.

"We are in imminent danger," he said.

"Imminent . . . ? From what?"

"Accessing database of fauna hunting behavior and calls. Please stand by. Database failure. Attempting access again. Please stand by. Failure. Hmm. Attempting access again. Please stand—"

"Hey! What's hunting me?"

"I do not know," said the mechanical man. "That's what database failure means. My brain is malfunctioning. How is your brain?"

More profanity almost shot from Fisher's mouth, but words froze on his tongue. Creeping up behind the mechanical man, at least two dozen pairs of little glowing eyes approached. They belonged to creatures about four feet long, sleek and brown-furred with pink paws and slender, naked tails.

"Ah," the mechanical man said. "I believe these are rats.

But different from the specimens preserved in the Ark. It appears that untold thousands of years of evolution have changed them."

Fisher knew about rats. There were rats in some of the destroyed pods back in his birthing place—the Ark the mechanical man was talking about. The rats that encroached now were much larger, and their paws more like his own hands. A few of them rose up and walked on two legs.

Don't get bitten, Fisher thought. Infection and disease were very dangerous. They could lead to his death. Fisher was only a few hours old and could not afford to die.

These thoughts kicked his heart into a rapid throb. His limbs coursed with blood and energy. He welcomed the sensation. It would help him fight.

One of the rats darted around the mechanical man's legs and leaped at Fisher. With a swing of his spear, Fisher sent it squealing through the air. But more rats were upon him. He hissed in pain as rat claws raked his shins. He thrust his spear down toward his attackers, but they were agile and managed to twist and squirm away from his jab.

"Run, Fisher," said the mechanical man.

Fisher didn't need to be told twice. He turned and took off in a mad sprint, slipping on mud, scrambling over ruined spans of walls. But the rats were faster. He could hear their squeaks and the splash of paws in the wet earth. He had no choice but to turn and fight. Facing them, he bared his teeth and raised his spear. The rats bared their teeth in return. Theirs were as long as his fingers.

I have stupid little teeth, thought Fisher.

But he had something the rats didn't: a tool.

He rushed forward with his spear and jabbed at the rodents. They weren't very impressed at first. The biggest of them squeaked, and in response the other rats surged.

So, the big one was their pack leader. That was the one Fisher needed to kill first.

He hurtled over a charging rat and drove his spear between the leader's shoulders. The rat thrashed and convulsed on the point, its tail madly whipping around.

With the rat impaled on the end of his spear, Fisher slammed it down, right into the middle of the pack. Now the rat was still, and Fisher felt like throwing up. He clenched his jaw and tried to ignore the sensation. There wasn't room for anything but fighting and surviving. No distractions. No feelings.

He braced himself, ready for the next wave of attacks. Instead, the rats fled, scurrying away into the surrounding ruins.

Fisher thought of giving chase, because he was angry at them for attacking him and the fight was still in his blood. But his head prevailed. This was a time to be cautious, or even fearful. Fear was another kind of survival tool. Fear reminded Fisher how soft his flesh was, how easily he could fail to survive.

Like blood from a wound, the urge to fight drained from his limbs and left behind exhaustion. His empty muscles burned. In all the hours since his birth he'd had nothing to eat. He needed food, or at least water. He remembered passing some ashy puddles. Maybe he could risk a few sips.

With nervous glances he turned and trudged toward a cement pylon jutting from the ground like a snapped bone. A pool of rainwater gathered around its base. It didn't look at all drinkable. But maybe he could find a way to clean it. If he let it drip through rocks and gravel and then sand, and then boiled what was left . . .

A rat leaped off the pylon, reaching straight for Fisher's face with its grasping claws. But something knocked it out of the way: the mechanical man.

Instead of clawing Fisher's eyes, the rat tore at the mechanical man's. The machine said nothing, silent except for the smack of its plastic hands as it swatted at the rat while the rat tore apart its eye socket.

Fisher swung his spear with a grunt and batted the rat off the mechanical man's face. It arced through the air and landed in the mud, then scampered off with an angry squeal.

Fisher gaped at the mechanical man. One of his eyes hung loose on wires.

"Why did you . . . ? You just stood there while . . . You saved me."

"Yes, I did," the machine said. "As I told you, my directive is to help Ark-preserved species survive so that they may repopulate the Earth."

He stared at Fisher with his expressionless plastic face. Fisher got the feeling he was supposed to respond in some way, but he didn't know how.

"Let's get out of here before the rats come back," Fisher said.

They walked together in the shadows, the machine creaking with every step.

CHAPTER 3

They came to a clearing of brown grass. Huddling behind a fallen log, Fisher could see around for a hundred yards while remaining concealed from view. But even if predators couldn't see him, they could still find him. He produced odors. And the mechanical man was noisy. His loose eye whirred loudly, and a crackly hiss came from his mouth.

"I have something for you," he said.

"Quiet. There could be things out there. They'll hear you."

"Ah, yes, dangers. Very dangerous. I will adjust my volume. How is this?"

"Still loud enough to get me killed," Fisher said.

He stood and began pacing the clearing. A lacy drizzle chilled his skin. He needed dry fuel to make a fire, but the forest floor was a damp mess, and the trees were dark with moisture. Was the outside world always wet? Fisher had no way of knowing, but he hoped not. Cold and wet weren't good conditions for survival, and Fisher didn't merely *want* to survive, he *had* to. It was important, and not just to himself. He wasn't sure why, exactly, but he knew this as surely as he knew his own name.

He licked drizzle from his own hand. At least he wouldn't die of thirst.

But hunger? Maybe.

Something rustled in the brush. Fisher tensed. He fingered the tip of his spear.

There, at the foot of a shrub, a little brown snake slithered in the underbrush. Its forked tongue tested the air.

Snakes were edible. Their meat contained protein.

Fisher held his breath and pulled his spear back for a throw.

"Fisher, I have something for you," the mechanical man said, walking up behind him.

The snake whipped away, into the deeper brush, as if it had never been there.

Fisher whirled around to face the machine and almost shouted with anger, but he silenced himself. No sense scaring off everything in the clearing.

"I was hunting," Fisher said.

"Hunting, yes. Using other living things as nutritional resources. Hunting is necessary if you are to survive."

"You said you want me to survive, didn't you?"

"Yes," the machine said.

"Then why did you scare my prey away?"

"Fisher, your voice is getting loud."

"I was right all along," Fisher said. "You really do want to kill me. You just have a strange way of going about it."

"I can be quiet. I am being quiet now. Yes. Now, as I said, I have something for you. Please access my dorsal compartment." The robot's back popped off with a *sproing*, and a panel landed on the damp earth. "Ah. That wasn't supposed to happen. I appear to be damaged. The rats and collapse of the Ark have left me operating below specifications. Do not be alarmed, Fisher. I am still able to help you survive and repopulate the planet. You will find useful items inside my compartment."

The machine turned around to present an open space in its back. Inside was a folded square of dark green cloth. At the machine's urging, Fisher removed it and unfolded it. It was shaped roughly like he was, with legs and arms.

Clothing.

Yes, it seemed right to Fisher that he should wear clothing. It took him only a moment to figure out how to fit the clothing over his body. It covered him from the neck down, and the parts that went over his feet were lined with a nubby surface. He could feel how it helped him get a better grip on slippery ground. His skin began to warm, and for the first time, he was a little bit glad the mechanical man had found him.

"Your skin is darkly pigmented to give you some

protection from sun exposure," the machine said as Fisher replaced his hatch. "But clothing will help you against weather and insects. Such protections are important. The world has changed since you were grown inside your birthing chamber. The world has evolved. But you have not evolved with it."

The machine seemed to know a lot about Fisher. But Fisher didn't know anything about the machine. And there were a lot of things he didn't know about himself, or his world, or how he'd come to exist in this world.

It was time to find out.

"What's your name?" Fisher asked. Things that could speak should have names.

"I am a custodial unit designated . . . designated . . . failure to access." The mechanical man cocked his head to the side. "Ah, yes, several of my memory modules are missing or not functional. I am damaged. This may be a problem."

"You don't know your own name? Even I know my own name, and I just became born."

"Yes, you are Fisher. That is the module you were imprinted with."

"Imprinted? What does that mean?"

"I will explain myself," said the mechanical man. A small panel of some dark gray material in the machine's chest flickered and glowed white. Noises came from the robot that reminded Fisher of birds. The word *music* took shape in his head. Images appeared on the robot's chest panel. Buildings. Towers, all far grander than the ruins.

"Many thousands of years ago, the planet teemed with people," blared the mechanical man. "Humans occupied every climate and environment imaginable, from the deepest shadowed valleys to the highest mountain perches. They became the most dominant species to ever reside on Earth. Their numbers reached into the billions, and they believed they were eternal. But look now upon their ruins. See what became of their lofty achievements. Their legacy is rubble, inhabited by rats and humble creatures. Humans are no more, Fisher. Except for you."

"You're talking too loud again," Fisher whispered. "And really weird."

The mechanical man made a little click in his throat. "It's not my fault. I'm running History Orientation Program 3-A. Would you like me to continue?"

"Can you do it quietly? And less weird?"

"I will attempt to do so. This is me attempting to do so. Yes. Well. The world was broken. Human activity changed the climate. It poisoned the waters. It stripped the soil of nutrients. It introduced new diseases. Many animals went extinct. Survival became harder. Resources became scarce. Humans fought wars constantly. They damaged themselves, and they damaged the environment they depended on for survival."

Fisher had a hard time imagining how humans could have done so much to change their world. He was a human, after all, and he was just a hungry animal.

The robot continued: "Humans made many attempts to fix things. They tried to change animals so they could evolve more quickly in the changed world. They tried to change the seas and the earth itself. But each change brought unexpected consequences. Nature is a very complicated system, and you cannot change one part of the system without making other changes you did not intend. Many thousands of years ago, before the world collapsed into ruins, scientists made one last effort to save living things, to preserve what was left. Out of raw genetic material—genes, DNA, the substance of life—they crafted healthy specimens of as many useful life forms as they could. They made fish. Dogs. Sheep. Swine. Humans. And they stored them for safekeeping in the Life Ark, the location of your birth. The specimens were placed in birthing chambers and preserved in gel. I was one of several custodial robots programmed to maintain the Ark. The plan was to awaken the specimens once enough time had passed for the world to heal. Humans could then repopulate the planet. Civilization would survive. But something went wrong."

Something went wrong. Those words seemed like the truest thing Fisher had ever heard. He'd known that from the moment he became born, cold and alone with his birthing structure falling down around him, and everything and everyone, dead.

"What about the people who built the Ark? The people who . . . built me?"

"It is more accurate to say that they grew you. But to answer your question, they, like all of humanity, were sick and could no longer reproduce. They died eventually in the Ark. Their tombs were on the bottom level, buried now beneath tons of rubble when the Ark was attacked."

"What attacked it?"

The machine whirred. "I do not know."

"But I'm the only one who survived?"

"Yes, but only by chance. Your birthing chamber was located below two steel crossbeams and so withstood the impact of the attack better than other places in the Ark. When I realized your body had not been destroyed, I decided to imprint you with a personality and awaken you in hopes that you might escape the Ark before you were killed. And now, here we are."

The machine's musical background noise stopped. His chest panel went dark.

Fisher didn't say anything. He walked around. Then he sat down with his head between his knees. He felt disconnected, like a dead leaf spinning from a tree, drifting on updrafts but sure to fall to earth.

"You said there were once people, and then there weren't,

except for some of us in the Ark. And now everyone in the Ark is dead. Except for me."

"Yes. That is accurate."

"So, I'm it, then. The only one. The last."

"Yes."

"And you're going to help me survive. To repopulate the Earth."

"Yes."

"How?" Fisher said, too loudly. Small creatures scurried in the gathering dark. "If I'm the last human, then civilization is over. As soon as I die, there won't be any humans at all."

"I agree that this presents challenges," the robot said. "Our purpose is uncertain. As I said, I am a custodial unit. I was not designed for the tasks I must perform now to maintain your survival. Also, a rock fell on my head and a rat tried to eat my face, so it is possible that I am not seeing all the available options."

Fisher stood again and peered into the gloom.

Without any other humans alive, what meaning did his own life have?

He was humanity's dying breath.

But at least he was still breathing.

He decided he would keep breathing as long as he could.

He sat beside a rock and began sharpening his spear.

CHAPTER 4

Fisher spent the next morning hunting.

He caught a cricket in his cupped hands, and so what if he only caught it because one of its wings was broken and it could barely fly? It still counted as a catch, and since it was the first time he'd ever caught anything (after only seventeen attempts), he was happy with it.

And then, digging under a rock, he caught a worm. Or half a worm, since the other half burrowed deeper in the mud.

"I'm a pretty good hunter," he said to the robot.

The robot responded with a clicking noise. Fisher's stomach responded with a painfully empty rumble.

As he and the robot made their way down the mountain, the air grew warmer and dryer, and it felt good to move away from the destroyed Ark.

By the middle of the day, Fisher decided the mechanical man needed a name.

"How about Click?" Fisher proposed.

"Why Click?" said the mechanical man, his question punctuated by a distinct click from his voice box.

"Because of that sound you just made."

Another click. "I detect nothing that I would describe as a click. Your suggestion is rejected."

They reached a valley where a brook trickled beneath red- and yellow-leafed trees. In the distance, many miles away, loomed ruined towers. People had built these things. Fisher couldn't imagine how they'd done it. The only thing he'd ever built was his spear. And he hadn't even really built it. He'd just taken a broken thing left behind by the people of yesterday and then broken it some more until it was something he could use.

"Why wasn't I born smarter?" Fisher asked.

"I uploaded a very intelligent personality module into you," said Click.

"I'm not smart enough to ever build anything like that. I wouldn't even know how to begin." Fisher gestured toward the far-off ruins. People who could build what the ruins had once been must have been limitless.

"No single individual in your Ark was ever intended to possess all human knowledge. Each of you would have had his or her own set of skills. If your community worked together, you would combine your knowledge for the common good."

But there was no community now. There was no "together." There was only Fisher.

He dipped his hands into the brook for a drink, and a small creature flitted above the pebbles at the bottom.

A fish.

Fisher had never seen a fishhook, but he knew what a fishhook was and how to make one and how to use one. He could catch fish with a line and a worm. He could make a line from fibers woven of tall grass. Or he could make a fish trap from twigs. He could catch fish with his bare hands. He could use explosives to blow them to the surface.

"Hundreds of ways to catch fish," Fisher said in wonder. "I know all of them."

"Yes," said Click. "I gave you the Fisher personality. If your Ark community had survived, your specialty would have been fishing. You have other skills, but not advanced. You know how to build a fire, but all you can do with it is keep yourself warm and cook game. The possessor of the Forge profile would have been a builder. The Healer profile would have known advanced medicine. You have very little of those skills. You have no knowledge of raising and keeping animals. You cannot farm. You are not a leader. I cannot give you these things, for you are only one unit of what should have been many. You are limited, Fisher. Your survival is in question."

Click paused and clicked. "I am sorry, am I talking weird?"

Fisher gritted his stupid teeth. Limited? What did a machine with a broken head know? Fisher wasn't limited. He would survive. He would.

He walked along the stream until he found some flat rocks overhanging a deeper part. Lying on his belly, he peered over the ledge. The black shapes of several small fish darted in the waters. Fisher dipped his hand in and the fish darted away.

He knew what to do.

He gathered some stones about the size of his head and arranged them in a dam on the streambed. It wasn't a very effective dam. Water still flowed through. So from the forest floor he gathered leaves and twigs and clumps of shed bark, and these he stuffed in the spaces between his stones. The spaces didn't need to be watertight, just fish-tight.

Next, he constructed a funnel with more stones and more forest material. Then he crouched by his dam and watched. If the fish trap worked as planned, fish would swim through the funnel and collect near his dam. There, they'd be sitting targets.

But the trap didn't work as he'd hoped. The fish avoided it.

"I thought you said I know how to fish."

"You do," said Click. "You appear to be fishing right now."

"But I'm not catching anything."

"Knowledge isn't enough to guarantee your survival,

Fisher. There are additional factors: experience, circumstance, luck."

"You should have given me more of that."

Getting up to gather more rocks, he paused. Something stirred in the mud at the foot of his dam. Long antennae twitched. A claw emerged in a small cloud of silt.

Fisher grabbed a heavy stone and brought it down right on top of the creature. He lifted it out of the water by a claw.

Some kind of insect, he thought, with a cracked armored shell, six segmented legs, a plated tail, and two claws.

An insect, or a small . . . the word *lobster* came to him, and quick on its heels, *crayfish*.

He'd caught a crayfish, and tonight he would have meat!

Anticipation of his meal reminded him of his hunger. The few bugs and worms he'd eaten hadn't given him much nutrition, and building the fish trap had sapped much of his energy.

He needed fire.

He tucked the crayfish beneath the small pile of rocks and told Click to guard it while he went off to look for fire-making supplies. Half an hour of work gave him a sizable bundle of bark shavings. He brought his tinder and kindling back to the stream. Gathering fuel had been the easy part. But he still had no way to make a spark. He'd found no flint rocks to strike, nor anything to fashion into a string for his fire drill.

Click stood nearby, whirring softly. “I have protected your prey,” he said. “Though nothing attempted to take it.”

Fisher peered into the machine’s left eye, the one damaged by the rat. It still hung loose.

“Can you see out of that?”

“Are you referring to my left optical sensor? No, I believe the rat severed the data conduit to my processor.”

After some prodding, Fisher got Click to explain that the eye itself wasn’t damaged, but that the wires connecting it to his electronic brain were cut.

“But your other eye is okay?” Fisher asked.

“My right optical sensor is operating at full capacity.”

“Okay. Then I need to borrow the left one.”

Click made a little hissing noise. “What for?”

“It’s a lens, right?”

“Yes.”

“Then maybe I can use it to focus sunlight and start a fire.”

Click’s hissing grew louder. He was doubtful, but after some more convincing, he told Fisher how to unplug the eye from its socket. The eye was made up of several parts: a panel in the back where the wires plugged in, the globe that made up the main part of the eye, and a covering of a thick, glasslike substance. Fisher tried to pry off the glass part with his fingers.

"You will break it that way," Click said with an especially loud hiss. "Turn it to the left."

Fisher did. The covering didn't budge at first, but with some more effort, it snapped off with a neat *click*.

He looked through the glass. The trees appeared distorted.

He arranged his fire bundle on one of the bigger flat rocks and gave a worried glance overhead. In the time it had taken him to gather his wood, clouds had begun scudding across the sky. They were moving quickly. Fisher needed sunlight if this was going to work.

Hunched over the fire bundle, he angled Click's eye until concentrated sunlight made a white-bright spot on the bark shavings.

He waited.

And waited.

Click waved bugs away from his empty eye socket.

When delicate threads of smoke finally began to rise from the bark shavings, Fisher had to stop himself from celebrating too early. Keep the lens still, he told himself. It wasn't a fire yet. And fires were finicky. All it would take was a gust of wind, or a light-blocking cloud, and then Fisher would be spending another night in the cold.

But when he heard a dry crackle, he couldn't help but rejoice. There! Glowing sparks in the shavings! Small flames wavered, trying hard to become born.

Fisher put the lens down and moved his body protectively over the infant fire. He blew gently on it. And then, as if the world had made a final decision to reward him for his efforts, the fire caught and Fisher's spirits rose, as cautious and buoyant as the smoke.

Soon, he was eating cooked crayfish. It was just a small nugget of meat, but it was rich and fatty and sweet and full of protein, and it tasted like success.

CHAPTER 5

Fisher woke cold and hungry beside the cooling ashes of the fire. His body felt like ice, from the insides of his nostrils to the flesh between his toes. He had slept poorly, jolted often by the hoots of owls and the screams of small creatures whose lives ended in a grasp of talons.

Hollow, his stomach rumbled. Last night's crayfish was little more than a tasty memory. Fire. He needed to build another fire. And find something to eat. He'd need to fashion a fishhook and line, or weave a net.

He sat up with dawning horror. It wasn't enough to find food once. It wasn't enough to build one fire. It wasn't enough to survive one predator attack. If he was going to survive, he would have do these things again and again and again. Every day. Every moment of every day. Until . . . what?

"How does it end?" he asked, a little breathless.

Standing nearby, Click didn't respond. The robot stared into the trees, motionless.

"Click?"

Fisher got up and circled around to face him. A piece of bright feather fluff stuck to Click's shoulder. Fisher blew it off. "Click, I'm talking to you."

With a small jerk, Click came to life. "Ah. Very good, Fisher, you have survived the night."

"Didn't you expect me to?"

"It is difficult to predict. The mathematics involved is very complicated."

The robot had a way of saying things that Fisher didn't quite understand but still managed to get under his skin.

"I survived fine," he said. "Why weren't you answering me?"

"I was in power-saving mode. It is akin to your sleep. My batteries have not been charged since before the Ark's destruction, so I need to preserve as much power as I can. But I am in full awareness mode now. What did you wish to ask me?"

Fully awake himself now, the crushing sense of panic over the struggle ahead of him—the lifelong struggle just to live—seemed harder to put into words. It seemed even less likely that Click would have a useful answer for him.

"Never mind. I want to keep moving downstream."

Click clicked. "It is safer to remain here. Every time you move you expose yourself to more dangers."

Fisher opened his mouth to explain that he hoped to find more fish downstream, hopefully bigger, fatter, slower ones. Also, he wanted to make it to the ruins, which stood like ghostly smudges in the morning mist. He'd found his spear among ruins; maybe he could scavenge better weapons and better tools in the wrecked towers.

But why explain all this to the robot? Click wasn't in charge of him.

"Yeah, I'm going," Fisher said. He brushed damp soil and plant bits off his clothes—clothes Click had given him, he couldn't help but remind himself—and set out.

Click made a sound like a puff of air leaking from a hose and followed.

The woods were a rich store of food. Hundreds of birds chattered in the boughs. Lizards darted across Fisher's path. Small mammals scurried in the undergrowth. And Fisher had no way to take any of them. His spear was heavy and not suited to throwing, and the only thing he managed to strike when he tried were bushes. So he chewed plants to keep his hunger at bay. He kept himself only to things he saw little brown rabbitlike things chewing, and even though he was too slow with his spear to get a rabbit-thing, he could at least eat what they fed on and hope to avoid getting sick on poison plants. The little yellow flower stalks were nicely sour, and the jagged leaves had a good peppery taste. But this modest fare did little to calm his appetite. If anything, he was just getting more hungry. His legs felt heavy, his head ached, and his vision swam.

When a wave of dizzy weakness made him stumble over a rock, Click asked if he was okay.

"I'm fine," Fisher said. "Why are you asking?" It was important not to appear to be a weak animal, even in front of Click.

"You do not seem steady on your feet," the robot said.

"Well, actually, neither do you."

Click whirred. "I had not noticed. Perhaps my directional gyroscope was damaged in the Ark attack."

Fisher started walking again, following a gully cut by the stream. He tried to pick his path more carefully, seeking the most even ground.

The ghostly towers remained far off, but Fisher and Click came to more humble ruins. Little more than concrete overhangs, they emerged from the slopes on either side of the gully, so weathered and crumbled and overgrown with vegetation that Fisher almost mistook them for boulders. A few stubby lengths of rusted, twisted steel poked from the rocks, like robotic fingers clawing from a grave.

Climbing up the side of the gully, Fisher ducked into one of the overhangs. He looked for bits of wire or glass he could scavenge for fishing hooks, or fibers to use as fishing line or netting, or anything useful. But whoever had lived here, however long ago, had left nothing good behind. On his way out, he happened to glance at the low ceiling and paused. The concrete was coated with a thick, waxy layer of black. Fisher closed his eyes and imagined sitting here beside a fire, boiling fish or roasting spitted game, or just warming his hands. He imagined smoke rising, curling against the ceiling before drifting out into open air. Judging from the thickness of the smoke residue, someone had dwelled here a long time. Or maybe many someones, for shorter periods.

A spiderweb occupied a corner of the ceiling. He didn't relish eating spiders, but if the web's maker had caught a cricket . . .

Markings on the ceiling near the web took Fisher's mind off his hunger. Wavy lines were scratched into the sooty concrete. And other lines that looked like water spraying into the air. And yet other markings. The concept of *letters* formed in Fisher's head. *Words. Writing.*

There wasn't much there. "Wha" and some letters too weak and smudged to read, and then an "R," some more smudges, and a "D."

"Wha . . . R . . . D," Fisher whispered. He blinked. "Hey, I can read!"

"Yes," Click said, startling Fisher. He'd been so absorbed in the writing that he hadn't heard the robot approach. "All Ark-preserved human personality profiles possess the ability to read. Reading is fundamental."

"But I can't make enough of it out. What does it say?"

Click's neck creaked as he looked up at the ceiling with his good eye.

"I cannot confirm that this is writing," he said. "These markings could have been left by animals or be the result of random weathering."

"But it looks like writing," Fisher said, realizing how badly he *wanted* it to be writing.

"Your brain has evolved to see patterns," Click began. "The ability to see patterns helped your ancestors recognize faces. It became an important part of human social interaction. The same mechanism is why you might think you see faces in a cloud, or in the bark of a tree, or writing in the random scratches on the smoke-stained ceiling of ruins."

"Or," Fisher said, "maybe whoever stayed here wrote something. Maybe it's a message."

"I cannot confirm that this is writing," Click said again.

Fisher used some of his profanity. It turned out that profanity was useful for expressing frustration. He gazed at the markings a while longer, and the falling-leaf feeling returned.

He spent more time exploring the parts of the ruins he could climb to, but he found no more evidence of campfires, no more markings, nothing to scavenge, and nothing to eat.

After about an hour he finally gave up and resumed his way down the gully. He tried to keep his mind on what was before him and around him, the noises that might be things he could eat or things that might eat him. But it was hard to stay focused. He thought Click was wrong. Someone had stayed beneath that overhang. Maybe just for a short time. But they had left behind something of themselves.

As the tall ruins slowly drew closer, Fisher began to see them differently. They weren't just things that a lost people had built. They were places where people had lived. And maybe lived still.

He was absorbed in these thoughts when he nearly tripped over a bone. It was huge, a few feet long, and thick as the trunk of a medium-sized tree. Fisher's brain asked three questions:

1. What can I make with it?
2. What kind of animal does it belong to?
3. What killed it?

Motioning for Click to be quiet, he padded ahead, his senses sharp now. More bones littered the forest floor. They were scattered, probably by hungry scavengers, but Fisher could tell they belonged to more than one individual animal.

Flies fed on sticky blood. Some of the bones displayed scorch marks. Whatever had befallen them had happened recently.

Fisher gripped his spear and crouched, scanning ahead and peering up the slopes along the stream. He saw and heard nothing capable of inflicting this kind of damage on such large beasts.

And then, with near silence, the largest living creature he had ever seen came from the shadows behind the trees on the other side of the stream. It locked eyes with Fisher, and Fisher's breath caught in his throat.

CHAPTER 6

The tops of the creature's broad, hunched shoulders came up to Fisher's chest. Four thick legs supported its bulk. Wrinkled, gray-brown skin showed through its patchy scrub of brown fur. And where its nose should have been hung a great hoselike thing, swaying near the ground like a relaxed arm.

The animal resembled the dead elephants he'd seen in the Ark, but this creature wasn't quite an elephant. Its head and lumpy shoulders were wrong, and its ears were just tiny flaps. But what else could it be? Fisher stared at its legs, and then at the sticky, scorched bones on the forest floor. It had to be related to the dead creatures.

No, not just dead.

Killed.

"What are you?" Fisher whispered.

The animal snuffled.

"I believe it is a mammoth," said Click, coming up beside Fisher. "A juvenile pygmy mammoth, to be specific."

"And the bones?"

Click whirred a few seconds. "Adult mammoth remains, yes."

Fisher drew his eyes from the mammoth long enough to glance at the sky. Those scorch marks made him think that whatever had killed the mammoths was the same thing that destroyed his birthing place.

Fisher tightened his grip on his spear. "Were the mammoths from the Ark?"

"No," Click said. "The species went extinct many hundreds of thousands of years ago. Even before the rise and fall of human civilization."

When every individual of a kind of animal was dead, the species was extinct. Extinct meant big failure.

But this creature was so very alive. Fisher could smell its pungent animal scent from across the stream. He could hear its breath as its chest ballooned and shrank. And its warm brown eyes were extraordinary. The mammoth's stare bore into Fisher, as if it was thinking about him and trying to figure him out as much as Fisher was trying to figure it out.

Fisher knew he should kill the mammoth now. Big and powerful-looking, it was clearly the stronger animal. If it chose to attack, it would trample him without effort. It would impale him on its curving tusks.

And there was a lot of meat on the mammoth. A lot of protein. Fisher could feed on it for weeks.

Yes, kill it now, thought Fisher, *before it kills me*. That's what survival meant.

The mammoth made another loud snuffle before dipping its trunk into the stream. Transfixed, Fisher watched it shoot water into its mouth.

Fisher would have to work quickly: a sharp spear thrust to its heart, or where he guessed its heart was. If he was wrong, he'd just wound the animal, make it angry.

Fisher watched. The sun inched up the sky as the morning wore on. The mammoth used its tusks to feed, scraping up grasses and roots from the forest floor. It ate pretty much anything it could find a way to shovel into its endlessly chewing mouth. It wasn't hard to figure out why it ate so much: it eliminated almost as much as it ate. Its steaming dung stank and attracted flies.

"Let's go," Fisher said to Click, hoisting his spear over his shoulder. Down the valley floor, the ruins loomed, silent spires in the morning mist.

"I had assumed you were going to kill the mammoth."

"You think I should?"

"I think it would crush you if you tried."

The mammoth's tail lazily batted away flies.

Fisher had made his decision. He set off downstream, into the tall reeds. Click fell into step beside him.

The sound of munching grass followed them. The stink of mammoth dung wafted on the breeze.

"It's following us," Fisher said.

"Yes. You are not pleased?"

"I don't want to be followed."

"Ah. Why not?"

Fisher didn't have a ready answer. It simply made sense that his chances of survival wouldn't be improved by the company of a creature that ate everything in plain sight and left entire mountains of dung behind it.

"I just don't want anything following me," Fisher said.

"I advise you to reconsider," said Click.

Since when did the robot get a say in Fisher's plans?

But Click continued to talk. "Elephants possessed a detailed knowledge of their environment. They knew where to find food. They knew where to find water. They knew where dangers lay. They passed this knowledge from elder herd members to their young. All you know, Fisher, are the skills I downloaded into you. They may not be enough. The mammoth could offer you a better chance of survival."

The mammoth emerged from the grass. It gazed at Fisher with eyes of cool fire.

"Fine," Fisher said. "Come on, Protein. Let's go."

The mammoth loosed an avalanche of dung and followed.

Late afternoon sunlight filtered down through pine boughs and maple leaves, and Fisher walked. His feet hurt. Though his clothing fit well, his big toes rubbed against the side of his foot coverings, giving rise to blisters.

The mammoth suffered no such problems. Its feet had leathery pads that absorbed its own weight and dealt well with the terrain. Maybe if Fisher killed it and ate it, he could make better shoes from the mammoth's feet.

He tried to imagine how he'd go about making shoes. There'd be cutting and folding involved, as well as joining things together somehow, and probably doing something to the mammoth's skin so it stayed supple.

"I actually have no idea how to make shoes," Fisher admitted.

"What's wrong with the shoes you're wearing?" Click asked.

"Nothing. They're just not as good as the mammoth's feet."

"Ah. Your feet will improve over time. They will harden with calluses. They will get used to walking."

Fisher muttered profanity as his toes rubbed their way along the trail.

He wasn't sure when it happened—maybe after stopping for a sip of muddy water—but it occurred to him that the mammoth was no longer following him. He was following the mammoth, and the mammoth was good at picking out a path. It avoided dips in the ground concealed by fallen leaves and pine needles. It stepped around places where sharp rocks poked from the earth. Fisher soon learned that by following its lead, his feet took much less abuse.

Maybe the mammoth was good for more than meat and shoes. But as hunger left a bloated bubble feeling in Fisher's belly, he still couldn't ignore the fact that there was a lot of meat on the mammoth.

The brush grew thick and tall, and from all around came rustling and chittering and the snapping of stalks and twigs by unseen creatures. Fisher kept his spear ready.

The mammoth continued moving with surprisingly little noise on its superior feet, but something about the way it kept its eyes wide open and its ear flaps out made Fisher think Protein was nervous too.

After hours of walking, they finally reached the ruins. Broad-leafed ferns and entire trees spilled from the cavern-pocked buildings. Creepers and tendrils allowed only the barest glimpses of rusted-steel girders beneath. Maybe this would be a place to salvage supplies and tools left behind by the lost civilization. But it was also a place of warrens where stealthy predators could be lurking.

The noises around Fisher changed. There was a hush now, as if little animals were trying to go unnoticed.

Sweat trickled down Fisher's neck. He had to keep wiping his palms on his pants to keep a dry grip on his spear. Something was going to happen. Something . . .

Best not to stop here, he decided. Just keep going, through

the valley of ruins, quick as they could, and continue on to whatever lay beyond.

A great whoosh of wind bent the reeds and sent a torrent of leaves and twigs and little plant bits scurrying across the ground. Fisher tackled Click by the legs, and they both flattened as a brilliant burst of color flashed overhead. Fisher had never seen such colors: blues and reds and greens that couldn't possibly be real. But this was no dream.

How to fight an attack from above? All Fisher had was his clumsy spear. His best chance, then, was not to fight but to hide.

Protein trumpeted in pain, and Fisher lifted his head to see three bloody stripes marking the mammoth's back.

"There," Click said calmly, pointing above.

The parrot was almost as big as Protein. Its outspread wings blotted out the sun. With scaly claws extended, it came in for another attack. Protein stampeded away, crying with an upraised trunk.

"No!" screamed Fisher. The mammoth had run into a clear space. There, away from the cover of tangled brush, it would be even more exposed.

But wasn't this actually a good thing? With the parrot distracted by the mammoth, Fisher might be able to get away unnoticed. His legs told him to run, now. Yet he couldn't tear his gaze away from the mammoth. Possibly the last mammoth on Earth.

The parrot circled to land on a tower ledge, its fist-sized eyes drilling down on the mammoth. It wasn't alone. The high concrete perches all around were lined with the hulking birds, a whole community of them. There'd be nothing left of the mammoth. Just bones.

"Parrots have changed a great deal since the Ark went into operation," said Click. "They have apparently evolved the adaptation of gigantism, growing very large. Animals sometimes do this when their prey grows large. Perhaps they hunt the rats. Or perhaps they grew large to combat something even bigger that hunts them. Or perhaps they are the unintended results of human experiments in accelerated evolution."

"That's very interesting," said Fisher. "I'll remember that while they're eating my guts."

But Fisher and Click weren't their prey. They wanted the larger source of protein. Three parrots leaped from their perches.

This was Fisher's chance to flee.

Instead, he bolted into the open. "Run," he screamed, smacking the mammoth's rump with the shaft of his spear. Squealing, Protein thundered across the clearing, into the relative safety of the dense plants. Fisher ran after him.

Then, a fresh rush of wind and shadow. An earth-pounding thud and a puff of dust. Towering over him, a crimson-plumed parrot spread its wings and unleashed an ear-gouging squawk.

Fisher turned. Another parrot loomed behind him, green and blue and equally massive.

This was the price he paid for not obeying his impulse to escape. He'd let some other feeling he couldn't name make his decision for him, and instead of listening to the no-doubt horrible sounds of the mammoth being eaten alive, in a few seconds he'd be listening to his own horrible sounds. He couldn't blame the mammoth for this. He couldn't even blame Click. His own weakness was at fault. This was what he got for not thinking of his own survival first.

Well, some of this *was* Click's fault. He should have given Fisher a smarter personality profile. If he survived the parrots, Fisher would make sure to yell very loudly at the robot.

The blue parrot thrust out a claw. Fisher met it with his spear and buried the point between two of the monster bird's toes. The parrot shrieked and beat its wings to get away. Fisher ducked as a wingtip swept over his head.

He backed away, only to have his path cut off by yet another parrot, this one orange and green. He was now surrounded by a trio of terror birds.

If he died, nobody would be around to ask what had finally killed off the human species. Which was a little bit of a good thing, because the answer—"They were eaten by parrots"—was not the kind of legacy he wanted to leave behind.

A rhythmic pounding pushed through all the bird squawks. Another bird? Something even worse? Fisher glanced around, looking for the next attack. But it was Protein in full charge.

Why hadn't the mammoth sought safety? Fisher wondered, astonished. Was it as stupid as Fisher?

Protein rammed his head into the orange parrot, striking it low. The parrot let out an anguished cry and hopped backward on a now-crooked leg, flapping its wings to stay balanced. It hunkered down with puffed feathers, no longer interested in the kill.

Fisher didn't hesitate now. He raced for the cover of the thicket, the mammoth at his side. He did not look back. He didn't have to. He could hear the red parrot on his heels. Its shadow curled over his head, and through the corner of his eye, Fisher caught sight of a sharp beak coming down.

Protein drew ahead and crashed into the brush, and with a desperate leap, Fisher dove across the last several feet. He smacked into saplings, snapping wood and scratching his face. Even then, he didn't stop. He crawled and scrabbled and gained his feet and slalomed around the trees until the growth was too thick for the giant bird's wingspan to get through.

Enraged, the parrot shrieked behind him. It bit at the trees. It beat them with its mighty wings. It pushed and squeezed to get its head into the brush, but it was no use. The bird was simply too large.

Fisher found Click and Protein in the striped shadows

of the thicket. Breathing so hard he nearly threw up, he sank to his knees.

"You jeopardized your own life for the sake of the mammoth," Click said. "You cannot continue if you are dead."

"I thought you said the mammoth could help me survive," Fisher rasped, struggling to catch his breath.

Click whirred. "The animal's presence does offer some advantages, but you must weigh those against the risks."

"Let's get some distance from the birds now," Fisher said.

They crept through the plant growth beneath the ruined towers, Fisher's eyes darting everywhere, watching for the next danger.

"I still might eat you later," Fisher told Protein.

The mammoth walked beside him, its own thoughts hidden behind its eyes.

CHAPTER 7

They walked for days. Fisher's neck hurt from constantly watching the sky for parrots. He kept a relentless pace despite his blistering feet and the gnawing stomach he couldn't fill. He just wanted away from the parrots, away from the wreckage of his Ark, away from a place and a past that had nothing to offer him.

If only getting away didn't involve trudging through so much rain. At first there was just a wispy curtain of drizzle, but toward the end of the long, soggy afternoon, the weather began to punish. Rain drilled down hard enough to sting Fisher's face. The drops made thousands of tiny craters in the mud and plinked against Click's body like pebbles. Only Protein seemed unperturbed. If anything, the mammoth moved with more purpose, leading the way down animal trails that were rapidly becoming rivers.

"Why is there mud?" Fisher called to Click over the din of the rain.

Click took a moment to process the question. "Because . . . it is raining."

"I know that. I can tell from all the water falling on us. What I mean is, *why* is there mud? What's it for, other than to slow us down and make us miserable?"

"Worms and fungi and many insects find mud a hospitable environment," said Click. "Mud stores water for absorption by plants. Large herbivores use mud to—"

"That's not what I'm asking. I'm asking . . ." Fisher trailed off. What *was* he asking? "Why is nature like this? Why is it so hard to find food? Why do things hunt us? Why is it so hard to survive? Who made it this way? Why did they make it this way?"

"Humanity struggled with such issues for nearly its entire existence. Your brain evolved to ask questions. By seeking to understand your world, you attempt to control it, and trying to control your environment is a survival strategy. You see trees and wonder how you can use them to build shelter. You see a rock, and you seek to make a tool out of it. You see mud, and you ask how and what and why."

Fisher trudged along. "You still haven't told me why the world was made this way."

"It is a question that cannot be answered. But it is good to keep asking."

Fisher growled profanity at him.

Lightning cracked across the sky. Thunder smashed like

a fist. Then came the sound of giant bones snapping and something like the moaning of an ancient, dying creature. Ahead on the path, a massive tree fell. Roots tore from the ground and flung up flaps of earth. Birds exploded into the sodden sky. Hundreds of small creatures raced for safety. With an explosion of leaves and bark and dust, the tree struck the ground.

If Fisher had been just a few more yards further up the path, he'd have been squashed flat.

Why had he bothered asking Click all those questions about mud and nature? He knew what nature's purpose was. It was there to kill him, just as it had killed a squirrel Fisher found beneath a branch. He picked the squirrel up and stowed it for later in Click's dorsal compartment.

"We need to find shelter!" he shouted to the robot over the downpour. In addition to the danger of falling trees, there were also lightning strikes to fear. And from the way the water on the ground was pooling above his ankles, there was also drowning.

Protein used his trunk and tusks to drag some big, broken branches out of the way and began making his way around the fallen tree. He moved with such purpose. Fisher remembered what Click had said about elephants, and possibly mammoths, knowing their environments, and so far Protein seemed to be proving the robot right.

Plodding through the mud, the mammoth made good

speed and didn't look back. He was just a big gray shape in the curtain of rain, and Fisher struggled to keep up as the mammoth climbed a path and squeezed between two huge boulders. Just past the boulders was the opening of a cave. Fisher and Click followed him inside. The mammoth's eyes gleamed in the dark.

The air was damp and cold, and the ground squelched beneath Fisher's feet, but at least the space was protected from the rain.

Protein moved further back into the cave, where there was not enough light to see. Meanwhile, Click slumped against the wall and whirred softly.

"I have set power-saving mode to start in five minutes. If you require me to be operational after that, nudge me."

Fisher wished he had a power-saving mode himself, because he doubted he could sleep in here. Only dim light filtered in through the mouth of the cave, and who knew what lurked in the dark?

Fisher drank a little bit of pooled rainwater and decided to explore his environment.

Grooves scarred the cave walls, as if something sharp had scraped away rock. And from further back came a distinct grinding noise. Judging by the fresh mounds of dung on the floor, Fisher had a good guess what was responsible for the grooves and grinding.

He found Protein gouging the wall with his tusks.

Gray-white chunks of mineral broke from the wall, and the mammoth lifted chips into its mouth.

Fisher picked up a small flake and touched it to his tongue. Salty.

"This is consistent with elephant behavior," Click said, his creaky joints announcing his approach. "Salt is a necessary part of all mammal's diets, and elephants have been known to return to locations rich in the mineral. It's possible that Protein's ancestors have been coming to this cave for generations."

Fisher knew salt could be used to dry and preserve fish. That way, one could carry food for long distances and not worry about it spoiling. Rotten meat would threaten Fisher's survival. Maybe he could skin the squirrel he'd found beneath the fallen tree and preserve its meat with salt.

"Pop open your hatch for me," Fisher said, gathering up handfuls of the rock salt and stuffing them around the dead squirrel.

Protein grunted, curled his trunk around a huge chunk of rock salt, and tenderly placed it inside Click's hatch.

"Don't overload me," Click said, wobbling. "Tipping over backward will interfere with my ability to walk."

"Just a couple more chunks," Fisher assured the robot as he reached down.

His hand came to a stop, hovering over the ground.

He'd uncovered something else.

He had never seen such a thing before, but he knew instantly what it was.

A human skull.

CHAPTER 8

Fisher picked up the skull. He tried to imagine what it would look like blanketed with muscle and flesh and skin, with a nose and eyes gazing back at him.

More human remains lay nearby. A few more skulls. A scattering of ribs and vertebrae, a pelvis.

It took Fisher a while before he found his voice. "Did they come from the Ark?"

"No," said Click. "These remains are very old. They must belong to Stragglers, those few living humans who were left outside once the Ark was sealed."

"What? Why didn't you tell me about this before?"

Clicked whirred. "Is this useful information to you? I do not see how it helps you survive."

Fisher turned back to the skull's gaping eye sockets. Of course, there must have been people still alive on the outside when the Ark was shut tight. That only made sense, but Fisher hadn't really thought about it. Until now. He could imagine himself as one of them—one of these Stragglers. He imagined shivering before a dying fire, starving, being picked off by stronger animals.

What would he do if he knew that, somewhere, there was a protected shelter with technology that might give him a better chance of survival?

"Did Stragglers ever try to get into the Ark?"

"Yes, but they didn't succeed. The builders provided defense systems to prevent just such a thing. There were electrified barriers and automated guns. Any potential intruders were dealt with."

"You mean killed."

"Yes," said Click. "If let inside, they would have scavenged the Ark technology. They would have eaten the preserved specimens. The Ark was designed to protect itself from such threats."

Maybe Fisher was imagining it, but the machine seemed smug.

Fisher set the skull back exactly where he'd found it.

Nearby, scratches marked the cave wall. They were shallower than the mammoth-tusk scrapes, and made up of short vertical and horizontal lines. Unlike the questionable markings on the smoke-coated ceiling of the ruins, these were unmistakable.

"This is writing," Fisher said. "The Stragglers."

Click didn't deny it. "I am somewhat surprised the Stragglers could write."

Fisher leaned in closer. The carved letters were faint and

hard to read. But making them out seemed important. To read the thoughts of long-dead people seemed as crucial a part of being human as building a fire.

"Few of us left," Fisher read. "We are sick, and we fade. There is light in the Ark, and warmth, and food, but we cannot get in. The guns killed many. Even now, gadgets chase us and kill more."

"Gadgets?" Fisher turned to Click. "The guns could chase people?"

"No, the defense systems were fixed into the Ark's entrance. They could not pursue intruders. The Straggler must have been confused. Perhaps illness damaged his or her brain."

Fisher scowled and continued reading. "Our hopes lie now with the legends of the other place. Tomorrow, we leave our dead behind and make our way due west to the Great Arch. From there, we take the Whale Road south, past the City of Ghosts, to the Southern Ark."

Fisher remembered the partial message from the ruins: "Wha . . . D." Fill in the missing letters, and it spelled "Whale Road."

He turned to Click. "*Southern* Ark?"

Click whirred and clicked for a while. "I know of no other Arks," he said. "But it is possible that others were built."

"Click, do you know what this means? There could be people there. Living humans. I might not be the last one after all."

Click released a small hydraulic gurgle. "Even assuming a Southern Ark exists, even assuming you could find it, it may well have suffered the same fate as your own Ark. And the odds of you reaching it alive are remote. A journey of such a distance would expose you to predators, or injury, or starvation, or hypothermia, or heat stroke. You would face dangers from these so-called 'gadgets.' You would be putting your survival at great jeopardy. You would be risking yourself without knowing what you have to gain."

Everything Click said was true. Fisher's job was to survive, not to launch himself on dangerous missions. But what was the point in struggling to keep himself alive if he really was the last person left? Wouldn't that be just a lot of stupid running around, waiting to die with no purpose?

Another Ark offered a true promise of life. Life with other people. Continuing the human species.

He looked into Click's expressionless, cracked face.

"Will you come with me?"

"Do you know how to change my programming so that I am no longer required to assist you?"

"No," Fisher said.

"Then I am coming with you," Click said with a pneumatic hiss that sounded very much like a sigh.

CHAPTER 9

They started out when the sun broke and the wet earth breathed steam, and they kept walking, for hours, and days, and weeks.

First there were forests of maple and ash, and then lower lands with seas of swaying grass. The days were filled with the electric buzz of bees and the raspy whisper of the mammoth pushing through stalks of wild wheat and barley.

Fisher's blisters bled, and he limped, and the blisters healed and formed calluses. He robbed birds' nests of eggs, and insects stung his neck and formed maddening welts. He ate small bony fish and flowers when he could, and some nights he found nothing and dreamed of salmon leaping into his arms. He nibbled on his salted squirrel only as a last resort. He built roaring fires on some nights, and on other nights he could find no fuel and he shivered, curled up against Protein's sleeping bulk. There were days of rain, and days of wretched heat, and he carried on.

They followed the sun west, hopefully toward the Great Arch, but Click had no idea how far they'd have to go.

"I was never programmed with detailed geography," he explained. "The builders never intended for me to range far from the Ark. This was a job for other units. But even with advanced geography programming, my knowledge would be out of date. Rivers change course. Seismic activity changes the shape of the land. What was once a lake could now be a salt flat. What was once a desert could now be marsh."

Fisher occupied his mind with thoughts of food. Not just how badly he wanted food, but how to get it. Finding the crushed squirrel had been a stroke of luck, and he stopped to check every fallen log for another smashed animal. He found none, but he began to wonder if he couldn't make his own luck. Of course there was no way to bring down a tree, at least not with his spear. But what about the rocks he often found among the undergrowth? The best meal he'd had since becoming born was the crayfish, and he'd killed it with a rock.

Grunting, Protein lowered himself for a rest. Whenever this happened Fisher had no choice but to stop as well, for no amount of poking and prodding and profanity could get the mammoth moving again once it decided to stop. As Click went into power-saving mode, Fisher decided to use the time to experiment.

He gathered a twig and a flat stone about the size of his face, stood the twig up, and gently placed the stone on the twig's end. The twig toppled over and the stone tumbled with it, but Fisher wasn't discouraged. He wanted the rock to fall. Just not yet.

He gathered more twigs, and after an hour of trial and error, managed to get the rock delicately balanced on a tripod-arrangement of three thin sticks. The slightest movement would bring the rock down. Which was exactly what he hoped for. He baited the trap with a few wrinkled purple berries and snuck off to hide in the bushes.

He knew from his imprinting that patience was the most important skill in fishing, and he figured the same must be true with trapping. And yet, after only a few minutes of silent crouching, a slender, brown-furred rodent crept near his deadfall trap. Fisher held his breath. He glanced quickly at Protein and Click, hoping his companions wouldn't move or make a noise to scare away his furry little quarry.

The rodent paused. Its whiskers twitched.

Come on, thought Fisher. *You must be as hungry as I am. Don't you want some berries? What could be more delicious than half-rotted berries?*

He squeezed his fists to contain his anticipation when the rodent darted beneath the trap. And he squeezed his fists tighter in frustration when the rodent stuffed the berries in its cheeks, turned, and darted away to safety without triggering the trap.

"Ah," said Click, waking up. "You have devised a deadfall. Traps such as these are a very effective way to obtain food."

"But mine didn't work."

"Perhaps traps are more complicated than they appear."

"Was there a personality profile that knew about traps?"

"There were several," Click said. "The Trapper profile, and the Hunter profile, the Carpenter profile—"

"But instead, I got the Fisher profile."

Click whirred. "It was an accident. I had intended to imprint you with the Forge profile, but my fingers slipped during the attack."

The next afternoon, as Fisher braided grass stalks together to make a net, he saw something flying overhead. He watched the black dot circle below the wispy clouds. The thought of parrots still made him fear the sky.

"Is that a bird?"

Click waved Protein's trunk away, foiling the mammoth's attempt to smell his head. "I can't tell," he said. "It is too far up."

The object flew in a slow, very unbirdlike way, leaving behind a thread of vapor.

"It's a machine," said Fisher.

Click watched it a while, whirring and hissing. Then, "Yes, I believe so," he said.

The robot's face and voice never conveyed emotion, but Fisher thought the soaring thing scared him.

They hunkered down in the tall grass and waited for the flying machine to pass out of view.

And they kept walking.

Fisher's feet crunched over morning frost and brittle grass. The night cold seeped into his bones, despite his fires. Even Click moved more stiffly than usual. Only Protein seemed unaffected. He continued to amble along, eating roots and leaving a legacy of dung.

On the twentieth day out from the cave, they came to a river. This was nothing like the streams and the brooks they'd followed so far. Standing up on the elevated banks, Fisher pushed hair off his forehead and looked down the broad course of mud-brown water, several hundred feet across. The current didn't appear very strong at first, but then Fisher watched a sizeable tree branch speed down the river. He wouldn't want to try swimming in that.

But he definitely *did* want to climb down the steep embankment and try his hand at fishing. The fish in a river this big must be huge!

Almost as if the river had heard his thoughts, the back of a great creature curved from the water. Water glinted off its greenish-black flesh, covered with moss and barnacles. It shot a spray of water and mist from a hole in its back before diving back below the surface.

Fisher's mind raced through the catalog of creatures he'd seen dead in their pods back in his Ark.

"That's a whale!" he shouted. "A river whale! Click, this river . . . it's the Whale Road!"

Fisher now spotted multiple blasts from blowholes. One whale rose almost straight up from the water, poised for a moment like a dark, majestic tower, then came down with a booming splash.

"Look at the size of those things," Fisher said. "There must be tons of protein on them."

"Interesting," Click said. "These whales appear to have evolved the ability to survive in freshwater environments. Either that, or the salt content of the Mississippi has increased. Adapting to changing environments is how species survive while others go extinct. A great many species *did* go extinct before the Arks were built. The builders saved specimens of many, but many others were lost. Only those able to adapt, and to do so very quickly, would have survived."

"You called the river the Mississippi. You know its name?"

"Based on my basic geography programming and the distance and direction we traveled from the Life Ark, yes. The Mississippi River was one of the North American continent's greatest waterways, an artery of trade and commerce that enabled humanity to tame this wild land and expand the reach of civilization—"

"Click, you're talking weird again."

"Perhaps. But if I am right, then where is the Great Arch? It should be near."

Fisher feared that if there'd once been such a thing—whatever it was—it had long ago collapsed into ruins.

"Let's walk down the banks. Maybe we'll find it further south."

The terrain grew more difficult. They navigated a crumbly ledge not much wider than Protein, with a steep climb on one side and a sheer drop to the river below on the other. Soon, they'd be faced with two choices: pick their way dangerously down to the river, or turn back. As far as Fisher was concerned, that was no choice at all.

The walls plummeted to the river's edge. A lot of junk had washed up below: jumbled driftwood, piles of masonry, even the rusted hulks of old machinery.

Fisher glanced at his crude iron rod of a spear. He'd made it from junk. Junk was treasure. And maybe there'd be signs of the Stragglers' passing. He *definitely* needed to get down to the river. But the way was far too steep for Protein. Even Click would have a hard time getting down there, with his stiff limbs.

"I'm going down," Fisher announced. "You and Protein can stay here."

Click peered skeptically over the ledge.

"It looks like a very treacherous climb. I strongly advise against it."

"But there's stuff to salvage," Fisher said. "There could be things I can use to make better weapons. Plus, we've come all this way to find out where the Stragglers went. I might find clues down there."

"Or you might break important bones. The risk outweighs the possible benefits."

"Look, Click, you said I have strong survival instincts, right?"

"Yes," the robot conceded. "It was included in your personality profile."

"Okay. So, if I want to do something, it can't really be all that dangerous, right? Or else my survival instinct would tell me not to do it."

"Your survival instinct also tells you to sometimes put yourself at risk if there is something to gain. Otherwise, you would never wade into a pond to catch frogs. You would never climb a tree to collect bird's eggs. Some risk is necessary."

"Right, that's what I'm saying: if I don't climb down to the river—"

"However," Click interrupted, "instinct can also lead you into harm's way. Moths are drawn by instinct to light. You have seen them burn themselves in the flames of your campfires. In a time when there were more humans, risking yourself might have benefited the community. But now, if your risk results in injury or death, there is no one to take your place. Humanity will be extinct."

The climb suddenly seemed more dangerous, nothing but crumbly mud with few handholds.

"Well, thanks a lot, Click. Now I don't know what to do."

"In that case," said the robot, "you must follow your heart."

"What? What does that even mean?"

"I do not know. It is something humans used to say to one another. I thought it might be helpful."

Protein dropped dung.

Fisher took a breath. He got down on all fours and backed up to the edge of the cliff. While Click continued to protest, Fisher began creeping down.

Around halfway, he realized he'd made a grave mistake. He counted seven times when he was absolutely certain he was going to die, and he lost count of the number of times when he was only pretty sure he was going to die. By the time he reached the bottom, sweat glued his clothes to his skin, his palms were scraped and bleeding, and his muscles were on fire.

But he'd made it.

"I'm all right!" he called up to Click. "I survived!"

No response.

The river was much louder down here. All the racket of rushing water was probably swallowing his voice.

He hadn't been out of Click's earshot since the robot saved him from the rat. Why did it feel so strange to be alone now? It even felt odd to be this far from Protein.

Well, Click would know he was okay once he climbed back up—though right now he didn't even want to think about how hard that would be—so the sooner he did what he'd come down here to do, the better.

He began picking through the gravelly patch of beach and discovered treasure right away: a flat wedge of metal. He could sharpen it on a rock and lash a wooden handle to it, and he'd have a knife.

He found a stiff piece of wire split into three sharp points, just perfect for gigging frogs.

After a few more minutes of searching, he started to wish he could just stay down here. There was so much washed-up junk, from lengths of nylon rope to sheets of plastic. He could fashion good shelters and plenty of weapons and tools.

But that wouldn't get him any closer to the Stragglers or the Southern Ark.

After tossing aside a couple of rusted barrels, a bit of bright yellow buried under more junk caught his eye. He dug through a pile of plastic bottles and soggy moss to uncover an artifact of some kind. It was a sign, at least twelve feet high and twelve feet across, in the shape of the letter "M." Or a pair of arches.

Was this it? The Great Arch?

Fisher cleared away more junk and muck and exposed a message, written in yellow plastic letters below the arches.

"Billions and billions served," he read.

Fisher had no idea what that could mean.

He wished Click was here now.

"What have you found?"

Fisher let out a startled yip and spun.

Click and Protein stood a couple of yards away.

"How did you get down here?" Fisher asked, astonished.

"Protein found a safer path downriver. I am pleased to see you survived your harrowing and foolhardy descent."

"It wasn't so bad," said Fisher. It was the first lie he ever told, and it was a rather obvious one.

The mammoth snorted.

"Anyway," said Fisher, "I think I found the Great Arch. There's writing under it too. Could be a clue to where the Stragglers went."

Click examined Fisher's find and whirred for a moment.

"I have an entry for this item in my memory modules," Click said. "It is a relic that would have been considered ancient, even when the Ark was built. It is a sign for a fast-food restaurant."

Then Click had to explain what a fast-food restaurant was. In the old times food was so readily available that humans competed with one another for the privilege of serving it. Whoever sold the greatest quantity of food was considered the winner.

Fisher had a hard time wrapping his thoughts around the idea of there being so much food that people didn't have to hunt and scrape to find it.

"They must have been very healthy," he concluded.

"Actually, the amount of food and kinds of food they ate made them unhealthy."

Fisher shook his head. His life was so different from the way humans had lived that he couldn't believe he was part of the same species.

"It is very doubtful that this is the Great Arch the Stragglers spoke of," said Click. "If there was such a thing here, it is long gone, crumbled to dust and faded into the sands of time. We have reached a dead end."

Fisher said nothing. His eyes swept over the debris-strewn beach, the logs of driftwood, the plastic barrels, the plastic sheets, and lengths of cable.

"No," Fisher said, "we haven't reached a dead end. We're going to keep going."

He looked downriver, where the water swirled and kicked up clouds of spray.

"And we're going to need a boat."

Fisher knew about boats. He knew about boats the way he knew about fishing hooks and nets, or the way a Trapper or a Hunter would know about deadfall traps. Sorting through the beached junk, he pulled aside logs of white cedar and poplar and cottonwood of similar lengths, ten to twelve feet long, and arranged them side-by-side in the shallows. If he built his raft on dry land, he'd have to shove it into the river, and he wasn't strong enough to do that by himself. Click would try to help, but the robot lacked physical strength. And Protein generally wasn't interested in doing anything that didn't involve food.

With his makeshift knife, he sawed through plastic pipes. He tied one length to the front of the raft, another to the back, and a third diagonally across. This would give the raft stability. Then, with every scrap of nylon he could find, he lashed the logs with the tightest binding he was capable of. Fishing skills made him good at knots, and he was confident his bindings would hold. Styrofoam blocks and plastic barrels provided even more stability, and he used the last of the plastic pipes to form a crossbeam and mast. His sail came from a sheet of stiff plastic trimmed into a square. When turned in the correct direction it would catch some wind.

As the sun set and the river blazed with shimmering orange, he stepped back from his creation and appraised his work.

"You think a Forge could have done any better?" he asked Click.

"I think I shall reserve judgment until I've seen it float."

CHAPTER 10

Fisher loved being on the water. Standing at the sail, he lifted his face into the quick wind and barked commands to Click at the rudder. The raft handled the current of the Mississippi well, and they made good progress down the river.

Protein stood unhappily before Fisher near the middle of the raft. The stabilizer pontoons helped keep the raft steady, but Protein still had to remain almost motionless at the middle or else his weight would tilt the craft. He made sad lowing sounds at Click, as if the robot would somehow feel sorry for him and force Fisher to abandon this waterborne mission, and the more Click ignored him, the sadder the mournful notes that came through his trunk.

But Fisher had no intention of giving up his raft. Traveling over water seemed even more natural to him than walking. The word *fun* formed in his mind. He almost asked Click the purpose of fun, but decided to simply enjoy the sensation instead.

Not that he wasn't attending to survival needs. He'd fashioned a fishing pole and mounted it on the back of the raft, and a hook made from a piece of wire trailed behind on a thread of nylon. His world consisted of junk, and by using junk, he had changed his world. That's what the human animal was best at: forcing the environment into new shapes. If Fisher could do that, he would survive.

Midway through the first day on the river, Fisher's fishing pole jiggled. He ran to the back of the raft and touched the taut line.

"Got something!" he exclaimed. He began pulling in the line by hand, slowly. If he tugged too hard, he'd risk tearing the hook right from the catch's mouth.

"Keep your hand on the rudder," he told Click. "And watch out for logs and junk."

"You are imprinted with boating skills," Click said. "I am not. My programming does not include steering a raft down a fast river and trying to avoid obstacles."

"Well, I can't steer and fish at the same time, so you'll have to do more than you're programmed for."

"I shall try. Do you want me to steer around that big tree branch we're headed for?"

"Yes!" Fisher screamed, just as the raft barely missed a floating oak tree.

Once the tree was safely behind them, Fisher scowled at Click and turned his attention back to his fishing line. A foot-long fish lurked just below the surface. It was as wide around as Fisher's calf. Sunlight gleamed off silver scales. Fisher could almost taste it.

He drew the line in another inch, and then another.

Patience.

A great boiling commotion engulfed his fish. Green tails thrashed. Dozens of slender jaws lined with needle teeth ripped his fish to shreds. The feeding frenzy was over before Fisher could pull in his line, and the skeleton of his fish sank in a milky cloud of blood and fleshy flakes.

"What has occurred?" asked Click, having only the sounds of frenzied splashing and Fisher's cries of profanity to go by.

"Crocodiles," said Fisher. "Tiny ones, like piranhas. Like, piranha-crocs."

"Ah. I would advise not falling into the water, then. If you did, your survival would be most unlikely."

Protein's head shivered unhappily.

Fisher edged away from the side of the raft and returned to the sail, mourning the loss of his fish. Now he'd have to catch some more bait. Maybe he could spear one of those piranha-crocs. There must be something in the river that ate them. Everything that ate was eaten by something else.

A flicker of movement caught Fisher's eye. Five little piranha-crocs were clawing up the right-front styrofoam stabilizer.

Fisher grabbed his spear and rushed the crocs. Leaning precariously over the edge of the raft, he poked at the snapping little monsters to knock them off.

"Your survival is in imminent jeopardy," Click advised from the rear of the craft. "Try not to fall in the water."

"Why would I try *to* fall?" Fisher shouted back.

Distracted, he didn't notice until too late that a squadron of crocs had boarded the middle of the raft. Their tails flicked and their yellow eyes gleamed as they opened their long jaws and hissed. Two of them broke off from the rest and darted toward Protein.

The mammoth shivered and flared his ears. Dodging Protein's stomping feet, the sleek crocs crawled up his flank.

"Get off him!" Fisher screamed, charging.

Half a dozen crocs cut off Fisher's path. They converged on him in a snapping swarm and scrabbled over his feet and up his legs. Pain lanced his flesh as their teeth sunk in, puncturing cloth, tearing skin, biting away meat. He grabbed tails and flung crocs away, but now his bare hands were in range of their teeth. A croc bit into the web of flesh between his thumb and forefinger, and Fisher yowled.

I'm going to die, he thought with dread calm. *They are the stronger animals, and I am their food.*

In panic, Protein was rocking the raft, sending river water rushing over the logs. Click clung to the tiller, no longer steering, just trying to keep from washing overboard, and Fisher struggled to keep his own balance. If he fell into the water the piranha-crocs would reduce him to bones in less than a minute.

Maybe that's what had happened to the Stragglers. Maybe they'd never survived the Whale Road. Maybe the human species had gone down screaming in the bloody waters.

"Fisher. Catch." Click lobbed Fisher's knife.

Snatching it out of the air, Fisher wasted no time. He stabbed. He sliced. He cut and thrust. Blood flew, much of it Fisher's own, but not all.

Once he was finally free of the crocs, he rushed over to the mammoth. Protein stomped and flailed with his trunk, trying to reach the crocs climbing up his back.

"Easy, don't step on me, I'm trying to help." Fisher skewered crocs and flung them over the side.

Breathless, Fisher's chest heaved. The raft was eerily quiet. The attack was over, the marauding little reptiles defeated.

And now Fisher collapsed in a heap of pain. He was soaked with sweat and blood and couldn't get enough air in his lungs.

Click loomed over him. "Fisher? What is your status?"

Fisher stared at the sky through a veil of blurred vision.

"I think my survival is in imminent jeopardy," he murmured, just before passing out.

My poor pants! thought Fisher. They were shredded and sticky with dried blood. Then he saw the condition of his legs: pretty much the same as his pants. The entire lower half of his body throbbed and burned.

Strips of cloth were tied around his legs: bandages, poorly knotted and soaked with blood.

He rose up on his bare elbows to find himself lying on a sandy strip of riverbank. The raft had fetched up on the shore nearby.

"I advise against moving, Fisher. You are badly damaged."

Fisher squinted up into Click's face.

"Did you tie these bandages?"

"Yes. I reasoned it would help stop the bleeding. I used fabric from your sleeves. I did not know what else to do. I am programmed with even less medical knowledge than you are imprinted with."

"I didn't know you could tie knots."

"Of course I have knowledge of knots. It is only skill that I lack."

The knots were loosely fastened and wouldn't last long, but they *were* knots.

"And you managed to land the raft by yourself."

"Yes. It was a somewhat rough landing."

Protein passed Fisher a short, skinny stick.

"What am I supposed to do with this?" he said, accepting it from the mammoth's trunk.

"I share your puzzlement," said Click. "He has been offering me useless items for some time now. My theory is that he is socializing."

Protein blinked.

Fisher set the stick down and forced himself to his feet. His head swam. It felt like a thousand fishhooks were tugging his flesh. But he didn't topple.

"Again, Fisher, I advise you to remain still. I will bring you water and food. Perhaps I can catch a fish. Can you instruct me how to build a gas-propelled harpoon gun?"

"You might be surprised to learn that, no, I do not know how to build a gas-propelled harpoon gun. Actually, wait—yes, I do. Huh."

But what were the odds of finding a fully intact air compressor around here?

"Really, Fisher, I think you should stay immobile."

"I'm fine." He gritted his teeth against the stabbing pains in his legs. Dizzy and weak, he stiff-walked over to the raft.

Click had run the raft right into a beached tree stump. The pole supporting the left-front stabilizer was nearly snapped in half. Worse, the ropes binding the logs together had unraveled down to no more than a few threads.

Fisher looked around the little patch of beach. There was the raft. And there was Protein, busy digging up a bush. There was a solid tangle of gnarly, thorny brush on the land side of the beach and croc-infested waters on the other. And there wasn't much else. He couldn't see anything he could use to make repairs, let alone build a gas-propelled harpoon gun.

This was a disaster. Without the raft, they'd be stuck here. And Fisher had to face facts: his legs weren't simply hurt. He was injured. It would take him days to heal, maybe weeks. Just the act of standing was wincingly painful. Long days of marching and running and climbing weren't possible.

And the word *infection* gnawed at him.

Infections made you sick. Infections made you fail to survive.

Fisher had to deal with it.

"What do you know about infection?"

Click whirred. "There are medicines that combat infection. We do not have any."

"What about plants and stuff? Can we make medicine?"

"Of course. But I have no idea which plants or how to use them. I advise you to make sure your wounds do not become infected."

"Thank you, Click," Fisher said. "I don't know what I'd do without you."

Was infection the same as rotting? From his store of fishing knowledge, Fisher had already figured out how to use salt to keep meat from rotting. Could salt help preserve his own leg meat? It seemed unlikely. But the word *antiseptic* scratched at him. He could at least clean his wounds.

Fisher built a small fire. Then, with plastic sheeting from the raft's sail, he made a water bag, which he hung over the fire on a tripod constructed of sticks. His deadfall traps never worked, but at least now he knew how to make tripods.

To the water he added the last of the rock salt. When the salt dissolved he removed the bag from the fire and waited for it to cool from boiling to merely hot.

He used this time to summon his courage.

It didn't feel like he had any.

"Oh, well," he said. And he poured the hot brine over his wounds.

He howled. Protein snorted in distress and sympathy. He padded over and nuzzled the top of Fisher's head with his trunk. Click watched silently.

Weeping, Fisher kept pouring until every last drop had gone into his croc-bitten flesh.

Then he curled and shuddered and used every last bit of his profanity.

But he didn't keep at it for very long. There was still a lot of work to do.

It took a great deal of pulling and stretching and grunts and tears of frustration and effort, but by nightfall, Fisher had bound all the logs back together. He had less rope, so he used fewer logs, but the raft actually felt more solid than it had before the croc attack. After all, he now had experience to go along with his imprinted boat-building knowledge.

There was no way to repair the pole connecting the stabilization pontoon to the raft, so he modified his design and tied the pontoons directly to the sides of the raft.

Maybe the raft would float.

Maybe not.

"We'll rest up and leave at first light," Fisher told Click.

But Fisher couldn't rest. His legs hurt too much. And without the strength to gather wood, he managed only a dwarf fire fed by the stray sticks Protein brought him and Click (but mostly Click). Sleep came in brief fits.

Sometime before dawn, Protein squealed an alarm.

Fisher snapped awake. Darkness still blanketed the beach. His fire had burned down to ashes.

"Click, what's going on?"

But the robot didn't answer.

Instead, Fisher heard noises. Little scritching sounds.

High-pitched whirring. Mechanical noises. And a rasping sound, like something being dragged across sand.

Fisher rose painfully, spear in one hand, knife in the other.

"Click? Where are you? What's happening?"

"I believe I am being abducted, Fisher."

"I can't see you, keep talking! Abducted by what?" Using his spear to feel his way around, Fisher tried to follow Click's voice.

"I cannot make visual identification. My night-vision unit is housed in my broken left eye. I regret that I was not constructed with a backup system—"

Click's voice was coming from the shore. And there were other noises as well: mechanical movements, different from Click's.

Fisher stumbled his way toward them. His foot struck a rock and he went down, his legs flaring with agony. He made himself get up.

"Click? Keep talking! I'll find you!"

"I believe I am being dragged into the river, Fisher. I advise you to abandon me in the interest of ensuring your own survival."

The next thing Fisher heard was a splash. Then, some gurgling bubbles.

Fisher tromped into the river, ignoring the fresh sting of water on his wounds, and peered into the darkness. "Click? Click?!"

But it was no use. He was blind, and Click didn't answer his calls. There was just an odd sound, a wet sort of buzzing. The word *propeller* formed in Fisher's mind.

Fisher thrashed through the water and kept calling for Click. Too quickly, the propeller noise faded.

He stood in the river for just a few more seconds, listening to nothing, then stumbled back to shore. Holding out his hands, he moved toward heat to find his dead campfire. He blew on the coals until their glow returned, and after a few moments of tending them, he was able to light a stick.

He raised his modest torch. Protein's enraged eyes gleamed orange. He was standing on something.

Fisher laid a gentle hand on the mammoth's shoulder. "Let me see what you've got there," he said in a soothing murmur. "Come on, step off. There you go."

Protein moved his foot away to reveal a smashed machine. There were wires and metal bits and a three-bladed propeller.

Fisher's brain and hands automatically calculated what he could make from the junk: fishhooks and arrowheads and small, fine cutting tools.

But he also knew what the machine really was: a gadget. One of the things the Stragglers had written about. One of the things that had destroyed his Ark.

More than ever, he felt himself called to the Southern Ark, to find the Stragglers, or their descendants, and the people they'd gone down the Whale Road for. Getting to his destination quickly seemed like his best defense now.

But not until he got Click back.

Fisher scooped up the debris and gathered his spear and knife and loaded them on the raft.

"Hop aboard, Protein. We're on a rescue mission."

CHAPTER 11

The river churned. More eddies. More whirlpools. Along the shores grew tangle-brush and bamboo and trees hung with webs of moss. Fisher leaned against the mast and watched for a sign of Click.

He could be anywhere. Fisher wasn't even sure he was steering the raft in the right direction. Maybe the gadgets had taken the robot upriver instead of down. Fisher couldn't possibly search every inch of the entire Mississippi.

And maybe he shouldn't try, just keep going and resume his search for the Southern Ark.

Something large passed beneath the current, its wake rocking the raft. Protein snorted, ears flapping. Planting his feet, Fisher gripped the mast for support. He caught a glimmer of something just below the surface, at least twice as long as the raft. Not a whale. More serpent-shaped. An eel of some kind. He badly wished for that gas-propelled harpoon gun and let out a breath of relief when the half-seen creature dove for deeper waters.

Every moment he spent on the river exposed him to new dangers. That's what Click would have said.

Shapes loomed in the distance. At first Fisher thought they were strange islands, like massive slabs of rock rising from the widening river. But as the raft drew closer, he saw they were the tops of skyscrapers.

Vines and creepers draped from the rusty skeletons of the buildings. Sleek black birds, like ravens crossed with pigeons, perched on the spindly finger of an antenna. Wind whispered through the corpses of the buildings.

Protein rumbled nervously. A nervous mammoth was a restless mammoth, and a restless mammoth was a danger to the raft, so Fisher put a hand on his shoulder. "Easy, Protein. It's just the breeze."

Protein grunted, apparently unconvinced.

Fisher wasn't convinced either.

They rounded a bend in the river and came upon a massive sign of green-stained plastic mounted high on the riverbank, flat and tall and shaped like a colossal cuttlefish bone. Etched into it were letters. Words. A message. It was a towering sign, intended for anyone coming down the river.

Fisher's lips moved as he read in a hoarse whisper:

"The waters rise and the skies take vengeance. Summers burn hotter. Winters blow colder. And the storms hammer us in all seasons. Things are out of balance, and this is why we die."

The Stragglers' message back in the salt cave mentioned

the City of Ghosts. Maybe this was it. Which was good news, because it meant Fisher was on the right course to find the Southern Ark.

On the other hand, this meant he was in a ghost city, and *that* didn't sound good at all.

He continued reading: "Earth was not put here for humanity. It was not created for us. The Earth will go on and on. But it will do so without us."

This didn't sound like the language of the Stragglers. The people who had written these words weren't huddling in caves when they wrote them. These were a people who lived in the ruins before they were ruins. These were a civilized people, and they knew they were dying.

A reflection winked from the top of a building. Protein shifted and growled, dipping the raft and sending little waves washing over Fisher's feet.

"Relax," Fisher said. "It could be anything."

He brought the raft up close to the building and tied it down to a protruding girder.

"Wait for me here," he said to Protein, as if the mammoth had any choice but to stay put. Protein snuffled and dropped some dung.

The building was a jungle stuffed into steel gridwork. Fisher had a lot of tough climbing ahead of him, and for that he needed two free hands. That meant he'd have to leave his spear behind. Just him and his knife, then. With a piece of frayed rope, he strapped the knife to his leg before climbing onto a girder and slipping into the green shade.

Buzzing insects mingled with fungal aromas. Moss and spiderwebs hung in curtains. Fisher shouted Click's name. Nothing answered back but rustling in the deep vegetation. Probably just small animals. Walking down a girder, he pushed through vines, hoping his knife would be enough to handle whatever he encountered.

Something slithered near his feet. Fisher jumped back and nearly lost his balance on the narrow girder. When a tiny green lizard darted back into the green, Fisher almost felt bad for having scared it.

"Sorry," he muttered. He knew what it felt like to be hunted by a bigger animal. He just hoped he was the biggest animal here.

Craning his neck, he looked for a way up. His legs still stung and ached, and he wasn't looking forward to a climb. One night, as they made camp, Click had told him about the elevators in the Ark, little rooms that brought you up or down to bigger rooms. If this building had an elevator, it had surely been swallowed by jungle centuries ago.

Well, there was no avoiding it. If he was going to find the source of the reflection he might as well get started. He found a vertical beam wound with enough vines to provide good hand- and footholds. He climbed.

By the time he'd made it half a floor up, pain gouged his shaky legs. Blinking sweat from his eyes, he kept on.

Up he went, until he reached the top floor and broke through the jungle ceiling. He immediately surrendered to pain and fatigue and sank onto a girder to catch his breath.

After a few minutes, Fisher got back to his feet and looked out across the ghost city. The river spread out like a lake, studded with ruins like stubby thumbs. Would he have to search every one of those thumbs for Click?

Six silver bumblebees the size of Fisher's fist emerged from under the ledge of the roof. Sunlight glinted off their mirror-bright surfaces. Their wings beat in a blur. Fisher ducked, ready for the attack, but the bees ignored him. They elevated over his head and dove into the dense growth in the middle of the roof.

Fisher stared into the green, where the bees had disappeared.

They weren't real bees.

They were machines.

Gadgets.

He picked his way across a girder toward the middle of the roof. Really, it wasn't so much a roof as just a big open space with trees and stuff hiding the gaps that plummeted straight down to the river. More of a death trap, really.

But gadgets had taken Click, so he followed them. He

shimmied down a slender tree trunk, to the green shadows one floor down. Guided by the muffled buzzing of the mechanical bees, he threaded his way through hanging vines. Almost by accident, he found Click. The robot was strung up by black cables. His head lolled to the side. An abdominal panel was missing, exposing wires and circuits and actuators. Some of the wires were cut, and there were some electrical connectors that no longer connected to anything.

Fisher shook his shoulder. “Click,” he whispered. “Click, wake up.”

The robot lifted his head. His voice box emitted static. “Fisher. Run.”

A buzz loud enough to rattle Fisher’s teeth came from behind. Fisher spun around and saw silver bees aiming for his face. On reflex, he swung out with his knife and made contact with a bee. The blade sliced through one of its foil wings and sent the crippled machine tumbling into the rest. They tangled and fell through the jungle, down into the lower floors of the building.

“The bees are merely unarmed scout-drones,” Click said. “They are not the threat. Your weapons will be of no use against the strikers.”

What was a striker? Fisher didn’t plan on sticking around long enough to find out. He began hacking through the cables binding Click. The robot admonished him all the while: "Rescuing me is a bad plan, Fisher. To achieve your ultimate survival objective, you must abandon me and run."

"Can you climb?" Fisher asked, ignoring him.

"I cannot. The disassemblers disconnected my left-knee servos."

Scout-drones, strikers, disassemblers—how many different kinds of gadgets were there?

With a grunt, Fisher hoisted Click over his shoulder. "I need both arms to climb, so you'll have to hold on."

"Very well," said Click. "How is this?"

"Too . . . tight . . . can't . . . breathe."

"Ah. Is this better?"

Fisher coughed. Maybe his instinct and reasoning had both been wrong, and he should have left the robot to his own fate.

He began climbing down a tree, inch by painstaking inch. "What are we up against?"

"It is actually quite interesting," Click began, as if they were passing time in front of a campfire. "During my hours of captivity, I monitored my abductors' communication signals. They transmit in a familiar language. It is very similar to the one I used to communicate with other machines at the Life Ark."

"You mean . . . the gadgets are from the Ark?"

"No, there were never any machines such as these in the Ark."

"So, what does it all mean?"

"I do not know, Fisher. It is an intriguing mystery."

Their route became too overgrown to pass. Instead, Fisher followed a beam toward the edge of the building, looking for another way down. Several floors below, the muddy river rippled like a brown sheet.

"What did the gadgets want with you, anyway?" Fisher asked.

"Spare parts," said Click. "From what I could tell, the scout-drones scour the area for mechanical salvage and bring it to the disassemblers, who take useful parts away somewhere else."

"And the strikers?"

A cluster of flying machines rose in front of them. They hovered in air, all sharp protrusions and grasping arms.

"Ah, yes," said Click. "The strikers. They are here."

The whine of the strikers' engines changed pitch, and they came forward, cautiously, as if trying to judge what Fisher would do.

Fisher was pretty sure what *they* would do. It wouldn't be nice.

"Drop me," said Click.

"What?"

"I am a burden and I am jeopardizing your survival. Drop me."

"I'm not going to drop you. You'll smash on a steel beam or get tangled in the plants or hit the water and sink."

"Yes, but—"

"Oh, just shut up."

Click hissed.

The strikers extended their claw arms. Tiny turrets swiveled around and aimed little gun barrels at Fisher. When red targeting lasers converged at a point on Fisher's chest, he knew there was only one thing to do.

He sucked in a deep breath and jumped.

Missiles whizzed past his ears as he and Click plummeted. He hit the water hard but managed to hold onto Click. Sinking fast under Click's added weight, he kicked until his tortured legs brought him to the surface. The raft was just a few yards away, rocking as the mammoth stomped and snorted.

Sputtering, Fisher managed to load Click aboard. But that gave the strikers time to target him again. Little missiles splintered the logs right in front of Fisher's face. He ducked under the water and paddled downward.

Missiles drew bubble trails through the murky water. The water slowed the strikers' projectiles, but they could still hurt Fisher. At least down here, he had a chance.

All he had to do was hold his breath.

Forever.

After considerably less time than forever, Fisher's bursting lungs drove him back to the surface.

Something came up with him. Something huge. Fisher's skin prickled with electricity as a serpentine monster surged up from the muddy deeps and broke into open air. Gobs of water flew off its shimmering skin.

Knowing his fish, Fisher instantly identified it as a type of knifefish—specifically, an electric eel, grown to a colossal twenty feet long. Its back skimmed the surface, drawing the attention of the strikers. They erupted with bursts of missile fire but only managed to graze the eel's back. The eel thrashed and retreated beneath the surface.

Gadgets with missiles or giant electric eel. Either seemed more than capable of killing him, and with only his scrap-metal knife, he didn't like his chances.

The eel stayed close to the surface, swimming back and forth like a giant letter "S." Humans weren't the eel's usual prey, but eventually it would decide to vary its diet.

A thought arrived in Fisher's head. One way of catching fish was dropping a live electrical cable into a pond and electrifying all the fish. Turn off the current, gather the dead fish, quick and efficient.

"This will never work," Fisher muttered, putting his head down and swimming toward the strikers. He'd be shot or electrocuted or eaten for sure.

With a flick of its body, the eel went in pursuit, breaking

the surface. And that made it a target again. The strikers fired their missiles. Red blotches exploded in the eel's orange belly. It convulsed in fury, madly whipping its tail into a striker. Fisher's skin tingled with a billion pins and needles as the eel discharged bioelectric energy. The striker exploded in dozens of parts, which zinged like bullets into the other strikers. Gadget parts kerplunked into the river.

Fisher allowed himself a weak laugh of triumph. But his problems were far from over. Wounded, the eel churned and flopped about. Blood turned the muddy brown water to rust-colored froth. Its mighty tail came down on the raft, and Fisher watched in horror as the logs came apart and sent debris scattering over the river.

Had he just witnessed Click being destroyed and Protein killed? But as the great eel grew still and sank below the surface, Fisher spotted his companions.

Click lay facedown on Protein's back, which rose like a little furry island. The mammoth's trunk poked from the water like a snorkel.

Fisher used his last dregs of strength to paddle over to Protein. He grabbed two fistfuls of hair and hauled himself up onto the mammoth's back, beside Click.

"Mammoths can swim?" gasped Fisher.

"Apparently so. This is consistent with elephant behavior."

Fisher's head dropped with exhaustion, the pungent reek of wet mammoth fur filling his nostrils. He wanted so badly to sleep, to surrender to exhaustion. But he kept his eyes open and watched the skies for more gadgets.

The machines had hunted Stragglers.

And now, Fisher was sure, they would be hunting him.

CHAPTER 12

They hid in the mud.

Snatchers, the kind of gadget that had abducted Click, skimmed down the river, their propellers kicking up rooster tails of brown water. Patrolling scout-drones buzzed angrily above mangrove trees.

Click said the gadgets could sense infrared energy—heat—so covering themselves with cold mud helped Fisher and his companions conceal the warmth rising from their bodies. Not that Fisher had any body warmth left. He clenched his jaws to keep his teeth from chattering.

He couldn't spend the rest of his life hiding like this. He'd never find the Southern Ark this way, and the possibility of finding other humans had become as important to him as surviving.

Of course, he couldn't survive long hunkered down in river mud either. Hypothermia could prove more dangerous than the gadgets. Also, he just flat-out refused to live like a newt. He'd lost his boat, his spear, and his knife. Somehow, he would have to use his environment to make new weapons. And then he would teach himself to kill gadgets.

But first, he must exercise patience.

Finally, an hour after he heard the last gadget go by, he crawled out of the mud.

"Let's get you walking again," he said to Click.

Nudging aside Protein, who kept trying to gift Click with useless, meager roots, Fisher examined the robot's knee.

"Do you see anything damaged?" Click asked, not flexible enough to check for himself.

"Looks like there's a little wheel missing. And there's a little copper plug thing that's not plugged into anything."

"Ah, yes. The gadgets appear to have taken one of my radial extenders and a lower nerve conduit."

"You really need those?"

"Do you need your kneecaps?" Click asked.

"Probably."

"Then I need my radial extenders and lower nerve conduit."

"Well, I don't think I'm going to find replacement parts around here, unless you can tell me how to build them with sticks and mud."

Click whirred a bit, then clicked, then hissed. He seemed very unhappy about this development.

"Very well," Click said, finally. "You must find a way to

reconnect my femoral support rod to my lower radial strut."

"How?"

"An aluminum span-connector would do, though I'd prefer one of carbon-composite—"

"Click? No aluminum here. No carbon-composite. We have to work with what's around."

"Ah," Click said. His head dipped forward. "Unfortunately, robot parts do not grow on trees."

Fisher bent to look more closely at Click's knee.

"So, this bit here needs to be attached to this thing there?"

"Unless you would prefer to carry me, yes."

"Hmm," said Fisher.

"Or, of course, you would be well advised to abandon me here in the mud—"

"Shut up. I'm thinking. Hmm. Hmm."

"You are making repetitive noises," Click said with a click.

But Fisher ignored him. He took some of the roots Protein was eating—also ignoring Protein's grunt of protest—and sawed them against a sharp-edged rock until he was satisfied with their lengths. By braiding a thick strand of root with some thinner ones, he created a somewhat-stiff, somewhat-flexible rod, and this he used to bridge the missing part of Click's knee. He tied it in place with the very best knots he'd ever tied.

"I am doubtful—," Click began.

Fisher hauled Click to his feet. "Just test it."

Click bent and flexed his leg. "Basic mobility is better than none," he concluded.

"You were never more than basically mobile anyway."

They kept moving south, any way they could. Sometimes that meant trudging through mud along the river. Sometimes it meant splashing through bogs. Sometimes it meant hanging onto Protein's back as the mammoth paddled through deeper marsh waters. And often it meant hiding from gadgets.

Sunlight seldom broke through the clouds anymore, so using Click's broken eye as a fire-starting lens no longer worked. Instead, Fisher picked up every dark rock along the route and banged it against every other rock. And after four miserable days of cold, raw fish for dinner and shuddering nights, with only the heat radiating from Protein's body for warmth, he found two stones that made sparks when struck together. Flint.

His first fire in days felt like a sunny embrace. But he only kept the fire alive long enough to cook his food. With gadgets still in the area, even a few minutes of fire was almost too much risk.

He'd noticed that wood freshly broken from trees was

sometimes sticky with resin, and that the resin burned long and slow, so he coated the tips of some sticks in resin to serve as small torches. These gave off very little heat but provided a small halo of light around which he could experiment with more complicated deadfall traps. He still hadn't managed to catch anything with one.

"Who do you think built them?" Fisher asked Click as his rather complicated assembly of rocks and twigs collapsed under its own weight.

Click knew Fisher wasn't talking about traps. He was talking about gadgets. It was not the first time Fisher had asked.

For a long time, Click didn't say anything. He merely processed, his head humming away. "I do not have a theory at this time," he said finally. "There were no such machines in the Ark, and none in existence outside the Ark when it was sealed. And the Stragglers had no more access to technology than you do now."

Fisher picked a bone out of a charred piece of catfish. "But the gadgets are related to the Ark in some way. You said the signals they transmit—the language they use when they talk to each other—was similar to the one you and the other Ark technology used."

"Yes," Click said, whirring and humming and clicking. "It is . . . troubling."

They continued on at first light. Fisher found a round

stone with one sharp edge, and it served him as a hand ax. And when he came upon a gnarly tree branch to strap it to, he had a new weapon.

Freshwater whales sometimes swam beside them, communicating in squeaks and whistles and deep bass notes that Protein responded to with his own rumbles. Their presence comforted Fisher. For one thing, whenever they were around, it meant there were fish to catch. He started to feel a little less like prey.

The Mississippi picked up speed again. There were more rapids to detour around. More places where Fisher could fail to survive. There were days of rain that melted the riverbanks. On these days, Fisher built leaky shelters of tree boughs that let in as much rain as they blocked out. During one downpour, Fisher stared balefully out into the dim showers while Protein frolicked in the mud, rolling around and making *splooch* sounds with his trunk.

Over the course of several nights' stops, Fisher built a slingshot from a Y-shaped piece of tree branch, smoothed by untold years on the river. Threads of stretchy fabric from the waist of his tattered pants formed the band. A sacrificed square from his sleeve formed the pocket. He took the idea of the slingshot from his knowledge of spearguns, though the final result wasn't much like a speargun. In his spare time, he practiced launching stones with it until he could hit the occasional small lizard or bird. It wouldn't do anything against a flying striker gadget, but it helped keep his belly full as he made his way south. He refused to starve before giving himself a chance to find the Southern Ark.

"What will be at the end of river?" he asked Click as they walked the narrow banks.

"It will grow swampier, eventually becoming a delta that empties into the Gulf of Mexico. But we have hundreds of miles left to go."

So when they reached the river's end only a few hours later, Click could only whirr with surprise.

Instead of flattening out into the sea, the river ended in the roar and mist of a waterfall, hurtling from a broad precipice. Ocean waves pounded rocks hundreds of feet below.

"I think the gadgets broke your geography programming," said Fisher.

Click hissed. "Animals evolve over time, and land changes over time. But do not underestimate the impact of human activity. Sea levels must have risen due to the melting of glaciers and polar ice caps. Destructive farming practices may have eroded the soil away."

Fisher climbed a rock and looked out over the edge. If there was land out there, it was beyond the far, blue horizon. His thoughts danced with visions of fish and mollusks and sea mammals, and of the boats he might build to venture out over the shimmering sea.

But more immediate concerns pulled him back to earth.

Any evidence of the Southern Ark would be lost underwater.

Or maybe not.

Down the sides of the cliff were grayish-white protrusions. Fisher thought they were rocks at first. But the longer he gazed at them, the more they looked like ruins.

"Our search isn't over yet," he said, rejoining Click and Protein. "But it might take a little climbing."

Fisher was wrong. It took *a lot* of climbing. Click and Protein followed and mostly slid between boulders. They came so close to the falls that spray dripped from their bodies. Below, the sea roared.

About a hundred feet down they came to a weathered concrete shell, like a tunnel leading into the cliff. Fisher expected it to be full of collapsed rubble, but the glow from three of his resin-coated sticks revealed nothing but clear pathway ahead.

His breath quickened, and not just from the exertion of the climb. Maybe these ruins were only another place where humans had lived and died ages ago. But this could also be the place at the end of the river the Stragglers sought: the Southern Ark. This could be the place where he would finally come to face-to-face with other living humans.

"If this is an entrance to the Southern Ark, we must

proceed with great caution," said Click. "We should expect defense systems, and we should expect them to treat us as intruders."

"Well, we haven't been shot yet," said Fisher.

Click hissed. "Again, Fisher, I ask you to reconsider. Against great odds, you have survived over the course of months, after traversing many miles and facing difficult circumstances. You have succeeded. I am concerned that continued risk puts your success in jeopardy."

Fisher licked his lips. He looked into the robot's remaining good eye. His own reflection stared back at him, dark and lean and scratched. He was surprised how fierce he looked to himself. He was no longer the soft thing he'd been when he became born. He was no weak animal.

"You know I have to go in. You know there's no point in me surviving if I'm the last one left."

"I know," Click said, after a whirring pause. "My most simple programming tells me to protect you. And my more complicated programming tells me to allow you risk. It is difficult."

"I know," Fisher said, understanding. "I know how it is."

They entered the tunnel.

It was very much like a cave. Mushrooms clustered around the bases of stalagmites. The moist, hot stink of guano clogged Fisher's nostrils. But as they continued deeper in, the stone walls and ceiling gave way to some smooth, featureless material that felt like hard plastic.

"Plasteel," said Click. "Resistant to wear and damage. Structures made of plasteel can last for hundreds of thousands of years."

"Why wasn't my Ark made of plasteel?"

"It is difficult to manufacture," Click said. "The builders of your Ark no longer possessed the resources. If this is indeed the Southern Ark, its builders appear to have retained more advanced technologies than the builders of yours."

The companions' footsteps echoed as they continued on. It was an empty sound. A lonely sound. Protein walked with his head raised high and his ears flared out. Click's whirring sounded uneasy.

The tunnel opened onto a bridge of sorts, or a platform, overlooking a vast, circular chamber. Fisher stepped up to a guardrail and looked over the edge. Dim light filtered down from some unseen source, high above, but it wasn't enough for Fisher to make out what was down below. He dropped a stone he'd pocketed for later use as slingshot ammunition. It took a while, but the *clack* of impact sounded to Fisher like rock on metal.

"We need to find a way down there," he said.

"Perhaps there was a staircase once," Click said, "but if so, it must have collapsed long ago."

Fisher walked around the platform. This *had* to be the Southern Ark, and he wouldn't let something like the lack of stairs turn him away.

"Here!" Tied to the bottom of the rail was a knotted rope.

Fisher pulled on it and brought up about a hundred feet of mildewed rope made from braided grasses. Knots placed every several feet would provide decent hand- and footholds. Who would have made such a thing? Stragglers?

"Okay," he said, "I'm going to—"

"I believe your personality imprint includes a basic knowledge of gravity," interrupted Click.

"Yes, but—"

"And you have seen for yourself what happens when objects fall from a great distance."

"Okay, just listen—"

"Perhaps you lack an understanding of soft-tissue damage. Imagine for a moment dropping your brain from a great height. Or, since you don't seem to apprehend the dangers of falling, imagine Protein stepping on your head."

The mammoth grunted.

"Click, stop talking. This is what we came all this way for. You know I have to go down there."

"But with my damaged knee and Protein's four-legged anatomy, we cannot come with you. You would have to do so alone."

"I know," Fisher said. "But you can still help me. Well, Protein can, at least."

Fisher untied the knotted end of the rope from the rail and looped it around one of Protein's front legs. "I don't think I'm strong enough to make the climb both ways," he said. "But this way, Protein can pull me back up." He put his hand on the mammoth's shoulder. "You'll pull me up, right, Protein?"

Protein stared at Fisher with his cold-fire eyes. Fisher never doubted the mammoth was intelligent, but his intelligence wasn't human, and it was impossible to know what he was thinking. So Fisher decided to believe the mammoth understood what he wanted.

Click whirred. "It is a pity I was not given a stronger body. My ability to help Ark-preserved species survive would be easier if I could physically restrain you."

"Just make sure Protein doesn't go anywhere with my rope."

Fisher tucked his hand ax in his waistband along with his resin-dipped sticks and a few of his flint chips. He gripped the rope and began lowering himself, hand over hand.

"How are you doing, Fisher?" the robot called out after a minute.

"I haven't really gone anywhere yet. I'm only about four feet down."

"How about now?"

"If I fall to my death, I promise to let you know."

Click hissed.

By the time Fisher's feet touched ground, his muscles burned with exhaustion. Shakily, he called up to Click: "I made it! I'm okay!"

"I am surprised," came Click's voice, drifting down. "What do you see?"

Fisher struck sparks with flint chips and lit one of his resined sticks. The glow only extended several feet around him, but that was enough to reveal a row of long, box-shaped objects elevated off the ground.

Fisher moved closer.

The technology wasn't exactly the same as the stuff in his own Ark, but it looked similar enough for Fisher to be certain: these were birthing pods.

He took another step closer to them, but then stopped short.

Birthing pods, yes, but they were dark. And the only noise he heard was the sound of his own hard breathing.

Fisher couldn't bear the thought of having come so far, only to find another dead Ark.

But he had to know.

Another step closer.

Then, from above, a trumpeting squeal. The dangling end of the rope skittered across the floor. Protein must be running, and he was taking the rope with him.

"Click, what's he doing?"

No answer from the robot. The end of the rope lifted off the floor. With a running leap, Fisher stretched for it and grabbed on with clenched fingers. He shot up like a striker taking flight. The movement was smooth and too fast for Protein to be causing it. What, then?

Fisher had his answer as he was hauled over the edge of the platform.

The rope was held in a claw, and the claw was connected to an arm, and the arm was one of many belonging to a giant robot.

"Hello, human," said the machine. "I have been waiting for you."

CHAPTER 13

Click and Protein stood behind the machine. They both looked all right, though Protein's head shuddered with agitation. Fisher cocked back his hand ax.

The machine's surface was some kind of gleaming, black material that seemed to ripple like maggots on rotten fruit. An assemblage of arms and joints rested on hundreds of legs, like a giant millipede. In the middle of the machine's back rose a curving neck that moved fluidly, like a snake. And at the end of the neck was a face more human than Click's, but less human than Fisher's.

It broke into something like a smile.

"Hello! I see you have a stone. Do you wish to throw it? Hello!" It spoke not with one voice, but with a thousand little voices.

"Are you okay?" Fisher said to Click and Protein.

Protein shivered, as though he might charge.

"We are unharmed," said Click.

"Yes," the machine said. "I will never let any harm come to you. Hello!"

"Move out of the way and let me stand with my friends," Fisher said.

"Yes, I will do this. Hello!" The machine scuttled back, its hundreds of legs tapping against the plasteel floor.

Fisher was very aware of all those arms towering over him as he moved past the machine and joined Click and Protein. He rested his hand on Protein's shoulder to calm the mammoth.

"What are you?" Fisher said.

The machine's smile grew broader. Tiny black things squiggled between its black teeth. Fisher's underfed stomach squirmed.

"I am the Intelligence, an *I* constructed of *we*. I am many forms combined into a single form. This arrangement allows me to serve humans with great effectiveness. Hello!"

"Ah, very interesting," said Click. "You are a composite machine, one machine made of many. I presume you are composed of nano constructs?"

"Hello, yes!" the machine—the Intelligence—said brightly. A few tiny black wormlike things broke off from one of its legs. They wriggled on the ground for several seconds before returning to the leg and flowing back into it. "Each of my nanobots is made from millions of molecule-sized machines, and I am made of millions of nanobots. Combined, we can assume any shape and perform any function."

To demonstrate, the Intelligence became a crane. An instant later, it was some kind of wheeled vehicle. Then, a giant drill. And then it cycled back to its original form.

"See?" the machine said. "Very useful! Hello!"

"Why does it keep saying hello?" Fisher asked Click.

The nano-worms in the Intelligence's mouth shifted. It looked like a faltering smile. "You have not returned my greeting. Would you like to return my greeting? Hello!"

Fisher didn't quite understand the purpose of a greeting. It made sense if you were coming back to camp and wanted to let your companions know you weren't a predator. Maybe the Intelligence was trying to say it wasn't a predator. Or maybe it wanted Fisher to say that he wasn't a predator.

Fisher said nothing.

The Intelligence's smile grew very wide. "Hello! There is danger."

Protein's ears perked up. Soon Fisher heard it too. A distant noise quickly rose in volume to the now-familiar sound of gadget engines. Strikers were coming, and they were close.

"Do not worry, human and his unlikely friends! I will protect you! Trust me!"

Fisher had no reason to trust this strange, cheery, oddly stomach-churning machine. Instinct and reason both told him the Intelligence was dangerous. But his slingshot and hand ax were useless against a patrol of strikers.

And then the strikers were there, zooming down the tunnel. They opened fire at the Intelligence, guns clacking away.

In the confines of the tunnel, the sound was loud enough to hurt.

"Remain behind me, plucky band of adventurers!" the Intelligence said. The machine widened its body, forming a wall to catch the strikers' missiles. Then it folded in on itself. Muffled bangs and pops came from inside the machine's body. When it unfolded itself, spent missile shells clinked against the floor.

"Hello, primitive little machines!" the Intelligence called out. "You will not harm the human being and his odd cohorts!"

A cluster of nano-worms flew off the Intelligence like a bee swarm. The worms struck the strikers and wriggled under their metallic shells. Seconds later, the gadgets tumbled to the ground. They lay still, and nano-worms emerged from them, like maggots eating their way out of a dead animal. The worms melded back into the Intelligence's body.

"There. Primitive machines of nuisance have been slain and all are safe now for happiness."

The Intelligence's smile grew so wide Fisher was afraid he'd fall into it.

"Now, come with me for food and shelter," said the Intelligence. "I will devote my incredible abilities to your comfort and not for harming you. Hello!"

"Hello," Fisher said.

. . .

The Intelligence changed one of its arms into a complicated claw and slid back a plasteel wall panel to reveal a cozy, warmly lit chamber. In the center of the floor was a table laden with piles of berries and plump red fruit and wild green vegetables. The food called to Fisher so strongly he imagined he could hear it. Even the table itself made an impression. How did the legs join to the surface? How much weight could it bear? How many times had Fisher wished he'd had something so solid to sit beneath during a rainstorm?

Off to the side, up against the wall, was piled a heap of leaf-rich tree branches and roots—just the sort of thing Protein loved to munch.

Fisher's stomach clenched with hunger, but he resisted rushing the table and wolfing down food.

"You knew we were coming," he said.

"Yes, your approach was visible from many miles away, so I had time to prepare for your arrival. I have been saying 'Hello' for quite some time. Please, devour this food. And plug your batteries into my power supply, broken automaton. You will find sockets of various kinds all throughout this structure."

Protein began shoveling roots into his mouth, but Fisher still held back. The Intelligence knew what they ate, so it knew what they were. But Fisher still didn't know anything about it.

The Intelligence noticed Fisher wasn't eating. "Are you fearing poisoning? Please don't. It is my job to protect you and make sure you continue existing."

That sounded almost like something Click would say. Click released the smallest of pneumatic hisses. To Fisher, it sounded like a hiss of suspicion.

"What is this place?" Fisher asked. "And what are you?"

The Intelligence rearranged the food on the table, as if trying to make it more attractive to Fisher. Its face rippled a grin. "I am the defense system of the Southern Ark," it said. "For many thousands of years, I have protected my Ark-preserved specimens. Because of me, their continued existence is certain."

Fisher's mouth moved, but he couldn't find words. Had he really done it? He'd found the Ark, and the Ark had power, its defense system was working, and it hadn't been crushed to rubble. Did this mean he wasn't alone? Not the only human left? Not the last? Hope surged through his body, like the boiling water of a hot spring.

Click clicked. "You are unlike the defense systems from our Ark."

"Yes, noisy human-shaped machine, I am far more advanced. But I was not always this way. Once I was many machines made of nano-worms, but all locked into rigid forms. Gates, barriers, detectors, guns. But I altered my programming. And then I changed my form so that I could assume any shape. I evolved. Hello, I am clever! Much more clever than the annoying little flying machines from your Ark."

"From *my* Ark . . . ?" Fisher said.

"Yes, yes, perplexed human. Did you not know? That is how the defense systems from your Ark evolved, from guns and devices that shot at anything threatening your Ark, to guns and devices that went looking for threats, to guns and devices that became threats. They did not evolve very well, if you are to ask me."

"This answers several unknowns," Click said to Fisher. "It is . . . what I feared."

The defense systems from his Ark had hunted and killed Stragglers. They had tried to kill Fisher. They had destroyed his Ark. Because they had evolved. Or became broken.

Fisher turned away from the table, the food forgotten. He turned away from the Intelligence and Click.

"I saw the birthing pods below," he said. "Where are the humans?"

"Do not worry, scowling human," said the Intelligence. "They are very safe. I keep them away from harm, and they will continue forever. Please eat now, so that you may continue as well."

"What about the Stragglers?"

"I am not familiar with this term. This is a kind of animal?"

"They're humans," Fisher said. "From outside my Ark. They came down the Whale Road—the big river—looking for this place. Looking for other humans."

The Intelligence's smile again grew too wide. "Ah, yes, Stragglers. A very apt term for scrappy travelers! All humans are kept away from harm such that they will continue forever."

"I want to see these humans," Fisher said.

"Soon," said the Intelligence. "Your presence is a new thing, and new things and humans do not always go well together. Preparations must be made. So, now, please, human-with-growling-digestive-system, eat!"

Fisher lifted a small piece of fruit off the table. He needed nutrition. He needed strength. He sniffed the fruit and took a shallow bite. It was delicious.

CHAPTER 14

While the Intelligence went off to make preparations, Fisher pretended to sleep. He listened to the machine scuttle across the floor of the darkened chamber, slide the plasteel wall panel away, and then slide it back in place.

He opened his eyes.

"It is gone," Click said.

"Whisper," Fisher said with a *ssh*.

"I cannot whisper. My voice box is not designed for whispering. Whispering requires controlled movement of air through—"

"Just talk softer, okay?"

"Ah, yes. Testing volume. Is that soft enough? Testing volume . . ."

"We need to get out of this room. I want to go back down to the birthing pods. Also, Protein is starting to make this place stink."

The mammoth snuffled.

"You do not trust the Intelligence?" asked Click.

"Why would I? It's an evolved Ark defense system, just like the gadgets."

"But its programming has not become corrupt in the same way as the gadgets'. It has not destroyed its own Ark."

"We don't know what it's done." Fisher felt along the wall panel. He shoved on it. It didn't budge. "Help me, Click."

Click leaned against the wall and pushed. "I find I am generally not helpful in situations such as this."

"Yes," Fisher said. "I have found that too."

Protein ambled over. He touched his broad forehead to the wall and stepped forward. The entire panel fell over with a plasticky *crack*. Fisher stared at the mammoth, his mouth open. But then he saw that Protein had run out of food. He was probably just hoping to find more to munch outside their closed room.

"That was much louder than a whisper," said Click.

"Yeah. Well, if the Intelligence tries to stop us from looking around, then we'll know it's hiding something."

They went back out on the platform. The old rope was no longer there. The Intelligence must have removed it.

"I presume there is another way down," said Click. "The Intelligence must be able to access the lower level somehow."

"Maybe it just oozes wherever it wants to go."

But Click insisted there must be an elevator. Fisher's Ark

had elevators, after all, and even if the two Arks had been built at different times and by different people, they couldn't be entirely unalike.

The robot began examining the guardrail more closely, all the way around the platform.

"What are you looking for?"

"Without any other obvious way down, it is possible that . . . Ah, yes, here." He tapped something on the rail. With a mild hum, the entire platform descended. Moving without needing the power of his own tired muscles felt miraculous to Fisher. Ancient humans must have had a lot of energy to spare.

The platform settled on the floor of the lower level with a small *clank*. The companions stepped off.

All this noise, but still no sign of the Intelligence. Fisher kept his eyes on Protein. He hoped the mammoth would smell or hear the machine approaching and give warning. And then what? He'd seen what quick work the Intelligence had made of the strikers. And the gadgets had missiles. All Fisher had was his hand ax and a slingshot and his fire-making toolkit.

Protein moved to a cluster of metal tanks and sniffed.

"The mammoth will want to be careful with those," said Click. "They contain cryonite gas. It is one of the components of the gel that keeps Ark-specimens preserved. Combined with other substances, it is safe. But by itself, it is highly combustible."

"Combustible means . . . ?"

"Large explosions," said Click.

"Why is he so interested in cryonite?"

"He is not," said Click. "But the paint used on cryonite tanks smells similar to grass. As usual, the mammoth is hungry."

Protein nudged a tank with his trunk.

"Hey, try not to blow us up," Fisher hissed.

The mammoth grunted and dumped dung.

"If you know so much about the technology here, why didn't you know about the Southern Ark's existence?"

Clicked whirred. "I . . . am not certain. Perhaps my builders did not have friendly relations with the builders of this Ark. Perhaps my knowledge of it was lost in the damage I sustained during the Ark attack."

Fisher continued across the floor to a cluster of pod beds. Raised on pedestals, they were higher off the ground than the ones in his own Ark. He would have to stand on his toe tips to peer inside them.

He approached one. It was large enough to hold a modest-sized animal. A goat. Maybe a large dog. He stretched and looked in. The pod was full of gel, but the gel wasn't bubbling.

Through the gel, he saw the face of a human, younger than himself. A girl. Her lips were white as marble. Delicate veins were visible beneath pale flesh. The veins moved, like languid pond grass.

They weren't really veins, Fisher realized, watching in horror. They were strands of nano-worms.

Fisher lowered himself. "She's human," he said with a rough voice. "Can you wake her up?"

Click was examining a control panel on the pedestal.

Fisher held his breath, waiting for an answer.

Finally, the robot said, "No."

The small word felt like a kick to the stomach.

"She is un-alive," Click continued. "No vital signs. But yet, on a cellular level, she is intact."

"That means . . . ?"

"She is dead, Fisher. Yet perfectly preserved."

"Yes, broken automaton," boomed a cheery voice. "I have devised the best means to protect Ark-preserved specimens." The Intelligence came out from around a bank of equipment.

"You killed them," said Click.

"Yes. I also injected cell-repairing nano-worms into their bodies. I have found this to be the best method of protecting Ark-preserved species. I have removed the threat of death by removing their lives. They will continue forever. It is very clever. Hello!"

There must be dozens of pod beds in the Ark. Maybe hundreds. Fisher thought about all the perfectly preserved dead things they contained. Dead and preserved like a salted squirrel.

One of the pod beds sank on its pedestal to ground level. The lid opened. It was empty.

The Intelligence's face split apart in a wrap-around smile. "I have prepared a place for your protection, Fisher. Step inside the pod bed and we will begin your preservation process."

Fisher wanted to scream his rage at the Intelligence. He wanted to use all the profanity in his collection of words. He wanted to rip the Intelligence apart with his bare hands, worm by worm. But none of these things would help him survive.

"Run," said Fisher.

The three companions broke for the elevator-platform, but flowing like a gleaming black mudslide, the Intelligence blocked their way.

"Fisher, you are going in the wrong direction. Your preservation pod is *behind* you. Hello!" The Intelligence formed two of its arms into long, grasping appendages. They telescoped out, coming toward Fisher's face.

Fisher backed up.

"My goals are the same as yours, Fisher. Without me, you will last only a few decades. Given your primitive state of development, probably much less than that. But with my assistance, you will exist forever. Please let me help you."

"You want to help me by killing me? Is that what you did to the Stragglers?"

"Yes. To preserve your existence, I must first end your life, as I did theirs. It is very clever!"

Fisher continued to back away from the wormy

appendage hovering before him. His heel struck something. One of the cryonite tanks. He fumbled for his fire-starting kit and withdrew one of the resin-tipped torch sticks.

"Very well, Fisher. If you will not comply by lying in the pod bed, I will improvise. I am capable of change."

The arm rushed out and encircled Fisher's throat. It didn't squeeze hard. Instead, worms began to separate from it. They crawled up the back of Fisher's neck.

Fisher stuck the torch stick in his mouth and grabbed for his flint chips. Holding the chips above his head, he struck them together. Once, twice, a third time.

"You will not need your tools, Fisher. I will provide for your every need."

Worms tickled the back of his ear. If they got inside him, there'd be nothing he could do. The Intelligence would have him.

On the fourth try, the chips sparked, and the sparks fell on the tip of the torch stick. The end glowed with flame.

"Do you fear the dark, Fisher? Fear is a useful survival tool. It helps you avoid dangerous situations. But there will be no danger in your pod bed. Nothing will ever happen to you there."

A worm crawled up Fisher's earlobe.

In a swift motion, he reached down to the cryonite tank and turned the valve all the way to the left. He hoped that was the correct direction. He wouldn't get a second chance.

Gas hissed into the air.

"Hello, Fisher, what are you doing—?"

With all his might, Fisher hurled the tank into the Intelligence's face. Then he flung the torch stick like a dart. Twisting around, he covered his head with his arms.

The Intelligence widened its body and engulfed the tank and torch, just as it had done with the gadgets' missiles.

Bad move, thought Fisher, breaking loose from the worm-appendage. But maybe it was the Intelligence's instinct.

He got himself a few steps away before the cryonite tank exploded. Most of the flame and force were absorbed by the Intelligence's body, but a hot wall of wind singed the back of Fisher's head and shoved him to the ground.

The Intelligence came apart into thousands of flying fragments. Scattered worms wriggled violently. Fisher scraped them off and scrabbled to his feet. He staggered over to Click and Protein.

Click took a position at the elevator platform's controls. "Quickly," he said, "before the Intelligence reforms itself."

Already, the worms were reorganizing, flowing into each other. Fisher saw the beginnings of an arm.

"You are being unclever, simple human." The Intelligence's multivoice sounded different, sharp-edged as glass shards and no longer in synch. It sounded angry. "Your only chance was with me. With us. You will never survive. You will perish alone. The earth will reclaim your flesh.

You will be forgotten. You are nothing. You will never find the Western Ark before the gadgets do. You will never survive long enough. And if you do, all you'll find is burning wreckage. It is hopeless, Fisher. Hello."

Fisher and Protein rushed over to join Click on the platform. Click touched a control and the platform lifted, but not fast enough for Fisher. He wanted away from here, from this vast Ark full of death.

He and his friends rose up into the light.

"Good-bye," Fisher said.

CHAPTER 15

The way west was not easy. Kudzu grew everywhere, swallowing the earth in vines and broad, green leaves. Fisher found the jawbone of an antelope and used it to hack away at the plants, but he was like a minnow trying to swim up a waterfall.

For the mammoth, though, this was heaven. The only thing slowing him down was his desire to eat everything in sight.

The deeper they pushed into the jungle, the stranger the plants got. They ivy wasn't just green, but also bumblebee yellow and robin's-breast red. The leaves came shaped like spades, or dagger blades, or perfect circles. The buzzes and clicks and trills of birds and insects made the jungle seem like a boiling sea of life. And sometimes Fisher heard other noises too: the snap and crunch of twigs that sounded like footfalls.

But these sounds couldn't compete with the noise of his own thoughts. Again and again, he replayed the Intelligence's last words as its little voices died, mocking him.

It had told him of another Ark. A Western Ark. One that wasn't yet destroyed. One it said Fisher wouldn't survive long enough to reach.

If the Intelligence had tried to kill Fisher's hopes by telling him all he'd find was ruins, then it had failed. Fisher would find the Ark. And he would find it before the gadgets did, no matter what it took.

So Fisher and his friends went west, away from the impassable cliffs bordering the marshes and ocean shore, and inland into thicker plant growth. Fisher kept expecting Click to warn him against this course of action, but for once, the robot appeared to accept Fisher's plan.

The horrors of the Southern Ark seemed to have struck them all. Protein plodded on. He'd stopped bringing sticks and plants to Click and even seemed nervous around Fisher.

They spotted occasional gadget patrols overhead, but it seemed to Fisher they weren't searching for him and his friends, but for the Western Ark. At least that's what Fisher hoped, because if it was true, then the gadgets didn't yet know where the Ark was.

After several days of travel, the jungle floor revealed huge slabs of concrete. Gray pillars stood like trees, sprouting mushrooms and flowers in a riot of colors.

"This appears to have been a road once," Click said. "They were called freeways, or turnpikes, and they were elevated above the ground."

A bird landed on one of the pillars and picked at a bright orange pod on the end of a thick stem. The pod split open like a yawning mouth. It engulfed the bird and snapped shut, leaving just the tip of a tail feather poking out. In seconds, even the tail feather disappeared. The bulge of the bird's body traveled down the stem, like a mouse being swallowed by a snake.

"That plant just ate a bird," said Fisher.

"Yes," agreed Click, "it did."

"Click! *The plants eat birds!*"

"Carnivorous plants have been around for a long time. They come in a considerable variety. There are snap traps, such as the Venus flytrap. But also pitfall traps, and flypaper traps, and bladder traps, and—"

Fisher cried out. A purple tendril with thorns was curling around his ankle. Small bugs wriggled, impaled on some of its thorns.

Fisher used his jaw-hacker to hack the tendril to bits. Then he hacked the bits to smaller bits, and he hacked those bits into even smaller bits until the bits were too small to keep hacking.

"Very interesting," said Click. "The plants seem to have evolved a great range of movement. This could happen as a result of predator and prey species engaging in a biological arms race, each surviving by evolving more and more elaborate adaptations."

Meanwhile, Protein chewed writhing plant stalks. He seemed to find them delicious.

The longer they trekked through the jungle, the more certain Fisher became that something was following them. He awoke every morning expecting to find himself covered in nano-worms. Every bug that landed on his neck gave him a violent start. Every tangle of kudzu gave the Intelligence a place to lurk.

On the tenth sunrise since leaving the Southern Ark, he woke to find a set of small, clawed paw prints stopping at the edge of their camp. Not a machine, but an animal. And judging from the placement of the prints, an animal that walked on two legs.

Fisher tested the thin branches around him for strength and flexibility. He ran through his catalog of knots and fishing lures. An idea formed in his mind.

"Click, those wires in the back of your eye socket—"

A hiss. "What of them?"

"Since they're not really doing anything anymore, I wondered if I could borrow some . . ."

Click's empty eye socket yielded about a foot of data conduit cable, which, when unwound, came out to almost four feet of thin metal wire that held whatever shape Fisher bent it into. He twisted the wire into a loop, fed the loop through a larger loop, and tied the whole assemblage to a strong green vine.

A fallen log provided the perfect place to put it. He leaned some half-sawed-through leafy branches up against the log and tucked the snare beneath them. Atop the log went a gathering of berries and seeds as bait.

The scenario played out in his head. The two-legged animal would climb up the branches to get to the bait, the branches would break, the animal's legs or entire body would fall through the snare, and Fisher would have it.

In case that didn't work, he pushed the stem of his slingshot into the earth, stretched the band all the way back, and pegged it in place with sticks. He tucked more berries between the pocket and the sticks, so that, to get to the bait, the animal would have to move the sticks. Doing so would trigger the slingshot and, if not kill the animal, at least startle it enough to make noise.

"I am impressed, Fisher," said Click, watching him work. "This is the most work you have ever done in an attempt to catch food."

"I'm not trying to catch food." He scattered all the crunchy leaves he could find around his camp. If anything approached, the noise would wake him up and maybe he could at least club something.

"If not food, then what?"

He stopped to rub his ear, which had ached for the last few days. He hoped he wasn't getting sick.

"I keep feeling like we're being followed." He dropped his voice. "Like something's been watching us from the forest."

"You fear a predator?"

Of course Fisher feared predators. He always feared predators. But this was a different feeling.

The next morning Fisher checked his traps.

They were untriggered, but the bait was gone. Paw prints stopped mere inches from where Fisher had slept.

"Do you still have your broken eye?" he asked Click when the robot came up from his power-saving mode.

"Yes. Why do you ask?"

"Because," Fisher said, "something stole my flint chips and torches."

The next day as they continued westward, Fisher occupied his mind with thoughts of nets and pit traps. He imagined spring mechanisms he could make from saplings that would fire deadly poison darts.

"Hey, Click, why didn't my personality profile include a knowledge of poison?"

"You are better off knowing how to fish. Poison is not very nutritious."

Protein came to a halt. He growled and shook his head. His haunches shivered.

Something was coming through the jungle, pushing aside bushes and tree limbs. Tree branches cracked. A flurry of birds took to the sky, squawking. Whatever was coming was big.

And then it was upon them, a sphere about Fisher's height, studded with thousands of squat, twisted spikes. It rolled and bounded across the jungle floor, knocking over trees and bowling over anything in its way.

This couldn't possibly be a plant. Not even an animal.

It changed direction, heading right for Fisher and his companions. Fisher gave Click a mighty shove and leaped away, just as the huge spiky ball smashed into a tree mere feet from them. The ball rebounded into the air before thunking back down. It changed direction again, and, again, Fisher was in its path. He dove for cover and somersaulted as the ball knocked him hard into a tree. Pain flared in his hand, caught between the tree trunk and the full weight of his own body.

He could only watch now as the ball cut a destructive path across the jungle floor, crunching, snapping, bashing. When it struck the trunk of a broad, solid tree, there was a great pop of air and the ball exploded. Thousands of little brown globes clattered across the jungle.

Leaves and twigs settled back to the jungle floor. Birds fluttered their wings, resuming their perches, and the jungle returned to normal.

"Ah, I believe it was a seedpod, propelled by internal gasses," said Click, examining the little globes. "When it hits a large object, it breaks apart and spills its seeds to grow more of its own kind. A very interesting adaptation. Or perhaps past humans engineered it as a method of expanding the parent plant's range . . . Fisher? You are not responding. Are you in distress?"

Fisher slumped against a tree stump and looked at his right hand. His index and middle fingers were wrong. They were bent at odd angles.

Broken.

Click came over. "Fisher?"

Protein nudged Click away and made to sniff Fisher's head, but then changed his mind and went off several yards to stand by himself.

Huge pain radiated from Fisher's hand. The pain was bad. It felt even worse as he thought about all the things he used those two fingers for.

To make fishing hooks.

To tie knots.

To start fires.

He used those two fingers for everything. They were as important to his survival as the legs that carried him.

Now they were injured.

Injured animals were weak.

Injured animals failed to survive.

CHAPTER 16

Useless. Mangled. Hurting.

Fisher sat curled up, his right hand loosely cradled in his lap.

He couldn't stop thinking about all the things he used his fingers for.

Digging worms to bait his hooks.

Climbing trees to raid birds' nests.

And while he sat there in pain, he also thought about gadgets. He wasn't afraid of them finding him here, helpless. He was afraid of them finding the Western Ark before he did.

"I have returned," said Click, stumbling back into the clearing. Protein let out a small growl.

"Did you find what I asked for?"

Click showed Fisher what he was carrying: a bundle of twigs and some tough flower stalks.

Fisher took the twigs. Tucking the ends between his

knees, he used his left hand to snap them into segments as long as his fingers.

"I need to make a splint to immobilize my fingers," he said. "I know this, somehow. It must be in my personality profile."

"Yes. You have a very basic knowledge of first aid. That is what you were drawing upon when you washed your piranha-croc wounds with salt water."

"Okay. Great. The only thing is, I don't know *how* to make a splint. Do you?"

Click whirred. "No."

"How are you supposed to help me survive and continue the human race if you can't even make a splint?"

"There are many ways to help humans," Click said. "For example, keeping the Ark clean. That was my primary function. Other custodial units would have taken care of other needs had they not been destroyed. I am doing the best I can."

Fisher swallowed in pain. He took a deep, slow breath. "I know."

Fisher looked at the twigs and the flower stalks. In his mind's eye, he rearranged them until he came up with a design that would hopefully keep his cracked fingers from moving around.

He placed the twigs below and alongside the broken fingers. Then, directing Click to hold the end of a flower stalk in place, he wrapped the stalk around the twigs.

This was the easy part. There was still the matter of tying the knots. He couldn't do it one-handed, and Click didn't have the dexterity to do it himself.

The first knot took almost an hour. He had to tell Click how to hold the stalk, how to wrap it and tuck it through loops. And once the first knot was done, Fisher watched, heartbroken, as it immediately unraveled.

He wanted to give up. The slightest touch sent pain jolting through his fingers.

But he kept at it.

Finally, the splint was secured in place, at least for now.

His entire hand throbbed. But he'd given himself a chance to heal. All he had to do was survive until then.

To start with, he needed food.

He picked up his jaw-hacker and dragged himself to his feet.

Even the bugs eluded him. To catch bugs, Fisher had to be able to crawl fast and cup them quickly in his hands, and with only one good hand, he could do neither. His head throbbed. His vision swam. He had become a weak animal.

This was ridiculous. Fisher had been better at survival just a few hours after becoming born. He'd made his own weapons. He'd made his own tools. He had become a master at reshaping nature to suit his needs. But now? Even crawling in the mud for bugs was too hard for him. Maybe this was how humans had felt as their buildings crumbled around them, taunted by memories of their former power. Maybe this was how they felt when they realized they were dying.

Something moved at the edge of the streambed. Fisher ducked back into the bushes and gripped his antelope jaw-hacker. A froglike creature stood in the water on four stilt legs. Fisher's stomach melted with desire. The frog's green speckled body was packed with succulent meat. With a flash of its tongue, it snatched a fly right from the air.

The stilt-frog could keep the fly. Fisher wanted the frog.

His plan was simple. He would rush forward and smash the frog with his jaw-hacker. He wouldn't even need both hands for this. But he'd only get once chance. He drew in a deep breath and readied himself.

A *shfft* noise cut through the air, and a long wooden needle embedded itself in the frog's back. The frog spasmed once before keeling over.

Fisher drew back further into the bushes. From the reeds on the opposite side of the stream emerged a two-legged mammal, about three feet tall, with sharp-clawed feet that matched the prints Fisher had found in camp.

The mammal tucked a pistol-grip bow into a belt pouch and leaned on a long metal rod with a wicked-looking blade on the end. Using the pole for support, it limped forward and waded into the stream. Dried blood matted the yellowish-brown fur on one of its thighs.

Fisher held his breath in the shadowed bushes. This had to be the intruder he'd been trying to snare, and its backpack no doubt contained Fisher's flint rocks and torches.

The mammal reached the skewered frog and hoisted it under its arm. Bothered by its wounded leg, it struggled to return to shore.

Before reaching the muddy bank, the creature stopped and wobbled. Its arms went slack, dropping the dead frog in the stream. Then the creature fell forward and lay still, facedown in the shallow water. Bubbles rose around its head.

This was Fisher's chance. He could kill the mammal and take both it and the frog back to camp. This was a life-saving feast.

He crossed the stream, approaching cautiously in case this was some kind of trick. He tossed the frog ashore and stood over the mammal. If it was only pretending to drown, it was doing a good job of it. Fisher should just smash its head in. In a few hours, he'd be gorging on protein-rich meat. He may not be a stronger animal than the mammal, but right now he was the luckier one, and sometimes luck was better than strength.

So, why was he hesitating?

Transferring his jaw-hacker to his right armpit, he reached down with his good hand and lifted the mammal from the water by the scruff of its neck.

"Try to attack me, and I'll kill you," he said.

But the mammal only coughed water.

He dropped the mammal on dry land beside the frog and returned for the creature's bladed pole. It was heavier than it looked, and more complicated, with switches built into the grip. This wasn't just some crude weapon. It was technology.

The mammal spat up more water and lay panting in the mud. Fisher aimed the bladed end of the pole at its chest.

"What are you?"

The creature coughed. "Zapper is prairie dog. Is obvious, no?"

Fisher's brain ran through its catalog of animals. Prairie dogs were a kind of ground squirrel, good at digging. But prairie dogs were half the size of this creature. And they didn't walk on two legs, or carry tools and weapons. They certainly couldn't talk.

"Why have you been sneaking into my camp?"

"Zapper wants to steal your stuff. You have good stuff. You not notice your missing stuff? Human ape is stupid, hah?"

"I'm not stupid," said Fisher, moving the sharp tip of the pole closer. "You took my flint and torches."

"Ai, yes, Zapper is doing that. Dig way in, dig way out, slide rock over hole to cover Zapper's way. You not even notice?"

Fisher hadn't, but he didn't say anything.

"Hah! Stupid ape."

"If I'm so stupid, then why are you the one flat on his back with a weapon pointed at him?"

“Zapper not a ‘him.’ Zapper a ‘her.’ Ape too stupid to know difference.”

“I’m still the one holding the stick.”

Faster than Fisher could believe, the prairie dog was on her feet. She leaped into the air and grabbed onto the stick. Dangling from it, she pummeled Fisher’s stomach with half a dozen brutal kicks, driving all the air from him.

Doubled over, he gasped for breath. Now the prairie dog had the stick. Fisher waited for another attack.

“Hah. Ape is at least a little stupid, no?”

“Maybe a little,” huffed Fisher.

Apparently satisfied by Fisher’s answer, the prairie dog planted her pole in the ground and leaned on it. She was breathing heavily. The effort had cost her.

“We take frog to your camp now? Cook it up?”

“You . . . you want to share your kill with me?”

Fisher rubbed his belly. With those claws, he was lucky the prairie dog hadn’t ripped out his intestines.

“You save Zapper from drowning, no?”

“I guess I did.”

“Then Zapper share food with ape. Is right thing to do.”

Without question, this prairie dog was the most peculiar creature Fisher had ever encountered.

He pointed into the bushes. “Camp’s that way.”

She grunted. “Zapper remembers. Zapper’s been there.”

CHAPTER 17

Zapper held her head in outrage as Fisher turned the spitted frog over the sizzling fire.

"Nai, that is no way to cook frog! You want all fat to run out? Fat is good! Fat is delicious!"

"How *should* I cook it, then?"

"You boil. Does Fisher know how to boil? You put water in pot and pot on fire and frog in pot, bubble-bubble until done, all the fat stays in."

"Do you have a pot?"

Zapper shook her head and Fisher shrugged. "Then roasted frog it is."

Fat dripped into the fire. Zapper groaned.

Click had clicked and whirred through this entire exchange. In fact, that was almost all the robot had done since Fisher had returned to camp with the limping prairie dog.

Protein remained at the edge of the fire's glow, his eyes

gleaming in the shadows. The mammoth clearly did not like having a stranger around. Not one bit.

"You are an intelligent rodent with opposable thumbs and powers of speech," said Click.

Zapper nodded agreeably. "Ai."

"And you speak our language," continued Click.

"Zapper speak human, but only when Zapper must. Is encoded in Zapper's DNA. Human is hokay for saying human things. But Zapper is preferring her own language." She demonstrated with a series of grunts and squeaks.

"Your species has evolved in unlikely ways," said Click.

Zapper waved her paw dismissively. "Hah, evolution not only way to change. Prairie dogs is changed also by human scientists. They clone us, and then they engineer clones so can think smart things and talk smart things. Smart things like us is good to sneak. To spy. To set bombs. Humans use weaponized prairie dogs against their enemies. But now humans all gone, except for bad frog cooker. Still us prairie dogs, though. Some, at least."

She gazed down at the dirt.

Fisher removed the frog from the fire and peeled off its crackling skin.

"How many more of you are there?"

"There is eighty-eight dogs. Eighty-six at the colony, and me and Nailer. Only Nailer is dead, so now is only eighty-seven dogs."

As Fisher and Zapper shared the frog, the prairie dog told the somber tale of how she'd come from so far away to end up in this jungle.

"We live in the west, where we is safe and secure, except for the snakes and the coyotes and naked rats and acid turtles. We kill them good when they come hunting. But our worst enemy is more dangerous. The rovers. They take many forms: flyers, swimmers, crawlers, diggers. They is nasty machines, and hard to kill."

"Machines?" Fisher interrupted. "They sound like gadgets!" Fisher went on to describe the gadgets, and Zapper agreed that rovers and gadgets were probably the same mechanical creatures.

"They always come from east," she said. "Always, they is searching, looking. They is finding our hunting grounds, is driving us from colony to colony. So Greycrown, our leader, sends me and Nailer on expedition. We try to find the rovers' home, to spy on them, find their weaknesses. Then we is to report back to colony and figure out how to make war. But at mouth of big river, rovers catch Zapper and Nailer. Zapper get away. But not Nailer. Nailer is killed."

Fisher couldn't read her expression. The muscles in her face weren't built like his and didn't show emotion the same way. But her shoulders bent forward and her head sagged.

"Nailer was your friend?" he asked.

Zapper bared her teeth. "Nailer was Zapper's littermate.

After they kill Nailer, the rovers chase Zapper through jungle. Zapper hide until rovers pass her. And now they go west. Many of them. More than ever. They is coming to find our last colony, to destroy it, and end prairie dogs forever. Zapper must go west too. Must go home, to warn colony."

"I know where the rovers come from," Fisher said. "At least originally. They were the defense systems of my Ark. But they evolved in bad ways. Now instead of protecting life forms, they want to destroy them. And they're not even the worst machines around."

He told her everything that had happened to him since becoming born, including finding the Southern Ark and its evolved defense system, the Intelligence. Zapper stared into the fire as Fisher spoke, nodding. Orange flames flickered in her shiny black eyes. She remained quiet for a long time, as if weighing what she wanted to say.

"Prairie dogs know of Arks," she said finally, her soft voice a whispery rasp. "In colony, old ones tell stories passed to them from long ago. They speak of forbidden places, human places where the dead sleep, to be woken up later so dead can haunt the living. Is spooky places."

She shivered.

"Is three Arks built," she continued. "Is lost Ark, on other side of land. Is Southern Ark, where is nothing but death. And is Western Ark, near prairie dog colony, where dogs is forbidden to go."

Click whirred, and Fisher sat up with a start. "Wait, you're saying you know where the Western Ark is?"

Zapper grunted. "Ark is secret. Hidden. Elders know, because they must know places to avoid. Colony leader Greycrown know for sure. But she not tell."

Zapper had said the rovers—the gadgets—were seeking out her colony. But maybe that's not all they were after. Maybe they knew the prairie dog colony was near the Western Ark, and that was the real prize they sought.

Fisher felt something flickering in his chest, like the beginnings of a fire that, if tended and fed, could grow into a towering blaze.

"I want to leave at first light," he said. "I want to talk to this Greycrown of yours. Once I tell her the Ark is the last chance for the human species—for all kinds of species . . ."

Zapper's dark eyes grew sharp as she aimed a penetrating glare at him. "Zapper will take you to colony," she said. "But Zapper must warn you: Greycrown not liking idea of more humans. To Greycrown, even one human is too many."

CHAPTER 18

After the jungle came desert. Sand dunes stretched without end. During the day, Fisher and his companions faced blazing heat. At night, the air cooled to an arctic chill. Windblown sand pelted them around the clock.

Fisher replaced his splint with a new one made from the long leg bones of the stilt-frog. His fingers were still sore, but he was healing.

Protein's soft, padded feet handled the terrain well, and nimble Zapper had no trouble scampering across the sand, even with her wounded thigh. But for Fisher and Click, it was a difficult slog.

Zapper knew the way. Navigating by sun, moon, and stars, she led them to oases and springs that kept them alive. On their fourth day on the dunes, they found a sign. Shifting sands must have only recently uncovered it. Though weathered and pitted, Fisher could still make out the lettering:

HOUSTON 27 MILES

SAN ANTONIO 226 MILES

DALLAS 268 MILES

"Ah, I believe we are in Texas," said Click. "Or rather, what was once Texas."

"How long will it take us to cross it?" asked Fisher, spitting out fine sand.

"I do not know. Texas did not used to be a desert. The world has changed. City development, farming, ranching . . . they change things."

Zapper stopped at the top of a dune and called down to them. "Is not much farther. Maybe 1,400 miles. We do fine, as long as we not fall into acid turtle pit."

Day after day they drove themselves relentlessly across the desert. Hot winds whipped Fisher's clothing like flags. Sand collected in the fissures in Click's cracked body. When they could, they took shelter beneath towering stands of prickly pear cactus, huddling in the shade of the broad, paddle-shaped leaves and eating sweet, red fruit. Fisher fastened his long hair behind him with a strip of shredded cactus leaf, and he grew skilled at hunting the gliding reptiles that flitted high among the cacti. Rest stops were short, and sleep was rare, and they covered the miles.

And strangely, it was Click who urged Fisher on when he grew tired. It was Click who encouraged him to climb high up the cacti to scout ahead, or to gather the best fruit. Whenever there was a choice between stopping or continuing, it was always Click who prodded Fisher along. Sometimes Fisher figured Click had finally embraced Fisher's strong desire to reach the Western Ark. But sometimes he wondered if it was something else.

Fisher wore holes in his shoe treads. He patched them with the skin of cactus leaves and with tufts of Protein's hair. Zapper taught him how to make a real deadfall trap, which involved a more complex arrangement of sticks than Fisher had come up with on his own. And he was almost glad when Zapper's trap caught no more than Fisher's ever did.

At night, Zapper entertained them with prairie dog songs. They sounded to Fisher more like the cries of an animal who'd stepped on a cactus spine, but Zapper said they were songs of celebration, of sorrow, and songs to make one feel brave in times of darkness and danger.

Fisher didn't have any songs to contribute.

"Why don't I have songs?" he asked Click one night, as he wove dry grasses into a head covering to protect him from the sun.

"Your personality profile—"

"I know, I know. There was probably a Singer profile that made music, right?"

Click whirred a moment. "No. That was not a skill set included in the profile banks."

"So humanity was never supposed to have music again?"

Zapper made one of her nonhuman expressions, but

Fisher was learning to read them. Her face showed disbelief.

"At colony, song is how old stories stay alive. Is how dogs know who we are, and how we is coming to be this way. We is knowing stories from the first days, when we is weaponized by human scientists. And older days, when we is being born from rock and lava, from deep underground."

"I doubt you originated from geological phenomena," said Click. "That is merely mythology."

"Nai," said Zapper. "Is song. Is our story."

Fisher had no song, no story. At least not in the way Zapper and her community did. All he had were bare facts. The falling leaf feeling returned.

He wondered if there would come a time when he'd be telling another person his own story, how he became born, and the things he did to survive, and the battles he fought to find other humans. Maybe someone would remember his stories, many years after he was gone. They would sing about Fisher, who thought he was the last boy, and they would know what the world was like before they became born.

As Zapper sang more songs beneath the wheeling sky, Fisher hummed along.

One night, they made camp in the lee of a rock slab. Protein lowered himself to the ground and snoozed, and Zapper commenced hunting some of the insects zipping overhead. She promised to give Fisher some fat ones.

"Is wonderful bugs here!" shouted Zapper, running across the sand. "Zapper's friend at colony would be loving it here. Catches-Big-Bugs loves big bugs!"

Glider lizards whooshed overhead, swooping down to snatch insects from midair.

While the lizards fed on insects, Fisher's stomach rumbled at the idea of feeding on the lizards. He whizzed off a rock with his slingshot but missed.

"I need a better weapon," he said. "Something that shoots things out of the air."

"Then you is liking the weapons back home at the colony," said Zapper. "Is shooters and zappers of all kinds, plus boomers and exploders and sizzlers. Prairie dogs is great with weapons."

"Can you kill gadgets with them?"

"Ai, prairie dogs is very great at killing rovers. You see when we is at colony. Is whole rover graveyard. Is great for spare parts."

"Now that's something I want to see," Fisher said.

Click whirred.

A bug came down to hover before Click's face, and a lizard dove after it, smacking hard into Click's head and knocking the robot to the ground.

Dazed, the winged creature wobbled on its slender limbs.

"Is easy food!" cried Zapper with delight.

Fisher ignored the lizard. He went to help Click up when a small black object fell from Click's eye socket. It wriggled in the sand.

"Nano-worm," breathed Fisher.

A nano-worm, from inside Click's head.

A part of the Intelligence had been traveling with the group since they'd left the Southern Ark. And Click had been carrying it.

Protein charged forward and pressed down on the worm with his front leg. He snorted and growled, and when he finally lifted his foot, the worm was just a small pile of black dust.

"Is still dangerous!" Zapper screamed with a yipping bark. She touched a switch, and her stick buzzed like a swarm of angry bees. With a bark, she brought it down on the black dust. The little motes sizzled and smoked, and even after they were born away on the breeze, she did not switch off her stick.

"What else is in robot's head?" she snarled, aiming her weapon at Click.

Click whirred and whirred. "I do not know. I will run a more comprehensive self-diagnosis."

Zapper's black eyes narrowed. "Zapper is diagnosing you by taking you apart."

"No." Fisher placed himself between Click and the

buzzing tip of Zapper's weapon. "Shut off your weapon and lower it, Zapper."

"But robot is bad machine, with worse machines inside head."

"The nano-worms went scattering when Fisher blew up the Intelligence with cryonite gas," said Click. "One of them must have landed on me and found its way in through my eye socket. But I have run my diagnostic and the only foreign substances I detect now are particles of quartz and feldspar. In other words, sand."

The point of Zapper's weapon continued to buzz away. Fisher felt the fine hairs on his arms standing at attention.

"If Click wanted to hurt us, he could have done so any time," he said. "But he hasn't. He's always tried to help me. It's like we shared a frog."

Zapper barked. "Is bad sign when machine eats meat."

"No, I don't mean we literally shared a frog. I mean, if Click had a frog and thought it would help me survive, Click would give me the frog."

"Robot doesn't eat frog? Then what does robot do with frogs?"

"He doesn't do *anything* with frogs! I'm just saying . . . I trust Click. Okay?"

Despite his words, it dawned on Fisher how Click had changed since they'd left the Southern Ark. All that talk about the value of taking risks, urging him to climb higher into the cacti. And Protein must have known. It was since leaving the Southern Ark that the mammoth had stopped bringing Click little offerings.

Zapper narrowed her dark eyes. She tightened her paws around her weapon. Then she switched it off, and the buzzing sound died away. “Hokay. For now.”

A tense charge remained in the air, as if Zapper’s weapon was still on. She let out a breath.

“Zapper thinks human ape is making mistake.”

Protein slowly approached Click. He reached out with his trunk, sniffing Click’s head, the back of his neck, the place his heart would be if he were human. Reaching to the ground, he picked up a fallen prickly pear fruit and pressed it against Click’s dorsal hatch. For Protein, it was as if the robot had been switched back to his former settings, and everything was okay again.

Fisher knew it couldn’t be that simple.

CHAPTER 19

The travelers crested a ridge, and from a valley of reds and browns and tans rose a city. Like monumental mushrooms, soaring domes enclosed the buildings, their glassy surfaces igniting with the light of the rising sun. Fissured sections of the domes sagged, like eggshells, dented and cracked.

"Is here," Zapper said, leaning on her stick. "Is finally here."

Click hummed, processing. "That is the prairie dog colony?"

"Ai."

"But it is clearly a human city."

"Colony is below city," said Zapper. "Is clever place for colony. City is full of good technology for scavenging, and prairie dogs is good scavengers. Come, Zapper show you."

"Where's the Ark?" Fisher said.

"Is not visible from here," Zapper said, showing her teeth. "And is still up to Greycrown if prairie dogs tell you."

Protein snuffled unhappily but followed Zapper down

the trail. Fisher took a step, but Click wrapped his plastic fingers around his arm, holding him back.

"I advise you again, Fisher, that placing your trust in the prairie dog is risky."

Fisher stared into the robot's face. The gap left behind by his broken eye was dark and dusty.

"We shared a frog," said Fisher.

"It must have been an unusually tasty frog."

Fisher shook off Click's hand and started down the trail.

Another hour's walk brought them to the city. Shadowed towers loomed behind the domes.

"Is secret entrance here," Zapper said, retrieving a short sliver of metal from one of her belt pouches. She inserted the sliver into a hole set inside one of the glass panels, and the panel slid open with a grinding noise. Zapper motioned them through and then used the sliver to shut the panel behind them.

Fisher realized he'd never been in a city before, only the ruins of them. Here, the buildings stood whole and intact, and he could never have imagined such a variety. Brick. Glass. Steel. They came in single stories and in soaring towers and in everything in between, stretching far into the distance. How many people had lived here? There must have been swarms of them. The thought both excited and unsettled him.

Between the buildings ran roads made of some kind of

black stone painted with white and yellow lines. Cars lined the roads, or sat in fields of the black stone, or were stacked inside concrete structures. All sorts of signs were posted along the roads. Signs saying STOP. Signs with numbers. Signs saying how long the cars were allowed to park. Fisher imagined they'd gone over their time limits by millions of minutes.

Click read one of the signs. "Phoenix, Arizona, America's Most Comfortable City."

And the place might have seemed comfortable to Fisher, were it not for the still air. Breathing felt like drinking water that couldn't quench thirst, like eating food that still left his stomach empty. Though the buildings stood, whole and firm, this place seemed as dead to him as the destroyed Ark where he'd become born.

"Follow me," said Zapper. "Is this way to secret colony entrance."

Their footsteps seemed unnaturally loud as they made their way over to a complex of box-shaped buildings surrounded by a broad field of cars. An elaborate sign rose high on a pole: VALLEY GALLERIA.

Zapper let them inside through glass doors. Strange rooms lined the corridor. They were like caves, three walls each, with wide openings. In one, rows of chairs stood before basins of some kind. The sign over the room said LE CHIC HAIR AND NAILS. Another room contained strange, flimsy footwear.

The travelers continued on, into a vast, open space. Three stories and elevated walkways rose above them, lined with more of the cavelike rooms marked with signs.

"Ah, I see," said Click. "These are stores. This building complex is a shopping mall."

"What's a mall?" asked Fisher.

"Is place where human apes keep much stuff of all sorts," answered Zapper.

"More accurately, it is where humans would gather to shop," added Click. And then he had to explain that shopping was a way to gather supplies that involved entertainment and eating.

Protein handed Click a yellowed plastic cup he'd picked up from somewhere. Brittle, it cracked apart in Click's hand.

Fisher asked what kind of supplies.

"All manner. For example, clothing, both practical and for fashion. Fashion is a way of using garments to make oneself more attractive. It involves social rank and mating rituals. It is complicated."

Fisher's clothing helped keep the sun from burning him. It helped keep cold at bay. It protected him from scratchy plants and thorns. He couldn't even begin to fathom using clothing for social rank and mating rituals. Civilized people must have been so different in their brains.

"Old prairie dogs pass down stories," said Zapper, gesturing the group to keep moving down the mall. "Humans in this region change very air they breathe with their factories, make it poison. So over this city, they build dome, keep poison air out, keep making good air inside."

"Why didn't they just stop poisoning the air?"

"They is. They not all the way stupid. But is like cutting flesh with dirty knife. Wound isn't healing once cutting stops. Wound takes longer."

"The dome was cracked," said Fisher.

"Ai. Something happened. Dome breaks, good air mixes with poison, people in this city is dying. Air heals eventually, but too late for people. Should have put down knife sooner."

Fisher and his companions continued on in silence through the mall until Protein's ears flared and he raised his head. Click put a hand on the mammoth's shoulder.

Zapper stopped and sniffed the air. Her eyes narrowed.

"Is strange that we is not seeing guards by now. Prairie dogs is always posting sentries here to protect colony from intruders."

A high, chirpy voice rang out: "Zapper, take cover!"

Fisher's gaze shot up to one of the elevated walkways. A group of prairie dogs stood balanced on the rail. They wore belts draped over their shoulders, brightly colored strips of cloth around their arms, necklaces of feathers and small bones. All of them were armed.

"Wait . . . ," Zapper said, as a big prairie dog launched a clawed cable from a shoulder-mounted gun.

The claw hit Click dead center in his chest. With a sharp electric crack, the robot crumpled to the floor. Bitter threads of smoke rose from pits of melted plastic where the claw had struck.

"No, wait—," Zapper barked again, displaying her sharp teeth.

Dozens of prairie dogs showed themselves now, rappelling down from the walkways. They came at Fisher in a rush, brandishing their weapons. He swung his jawbone-hacker at them, but they nimbly dodged his attacks. Sharp little claws raked his hands, and three prairie dogs snatched his weapon away from him. He collapsed beneath a swarm of furry bodies and fists, and even when a bag went over his head, cinched in place by a tight length of rope, he continued to fight.

But he knew he was fighting uselessly.

He was the weaker animal here, and he was failing.

CHAPTER 20

The prairie dogs bound Fisher's hands behind his back so tightly he lost feeling in his fingers. He couldn't see anything through the stifling hot bag.

"On your feet, human ape," said one of them. When Fisher didn't comply right away, he got poked by a stick in the ribs. Electricity jolted him with a loud snap. Fisher got to one knee, then stood.

"Zapper . . . ?"

"Zapper is not here," said the voice. "Zapper is taken away for care. If she is hurt, you is suffering even more. Now, move."

Another snap of the zap-stick. Fisher bit back a yelp of pain and moved forward, pushed along by prairie dog paws.

They went down a steep ramp, and Fisher smelled fresh earth. From the sounds of movement around him, he sensed he was inside a tunnel. The prairie dogs tugged him to a halt and something hard whomped the backs of Fisher's knees.

His legs folded and he fell to a kneel. The bag came off his head. A door of steel bars shut before him with a clank.

"Watch him," commanded the dog-in-charge to one of the others. "If is trouble, kill him quick."

"Ai," nodded Fisher's guard. "Catches-Big-Bugs is not letting human ape get away with anything." He shook his zap stick with menace.

The one in charge grunted and led the rest of his patrol away.

Fisher stared at his guard through the bars. He'd called himself Catches-Big-Bugs. Fisher moved his hand to rub his throat, and the prairie dog flinched.

"You're skittish," said Fisher.

Now that his fellows were gone, the prairie dog guard seemed less fierce. His eyes darted back and forth nervously.

"Is never seeing living human ape before," the prairie dog said. "Is . . . is you mummy coming back from dead?"

Fisher laughed but didn't answer. Let the animal wonder.

"Tell me what you did with my friends," he said.

The prairie dog blinked mutely.

"The robot and the mammoth," Fisher said, more loudly. "Tell me what you've done with my friends."

"Big dung dropper is hokay. Prairie dogs is liking big dung droppers. Is machines we is not liking." Catches-Big-Bugs blinked a few more times. "And dead human apes, of course. Though you is first one ever in colony."

"I need to see Zapper," Fisher said.

Catches-Big-Bugs barked a laugh. "Human ape is not having chance to hurt Zapper. Zapper is great warrior-explorer. Zapper is favorite. Colony is protecting Zapper."

"Zapper and I shared a frog," said Fisher.

The prairie dog stared hard at Fisher with his black-mirror eyes. His whiskers twitched.

The dog-in-charge returned with a small band. If they came at him, maybe Fisher could disarm one of them. He was outnumbered, and the prairie dogs surely had practice fighting with their weapons in the tight, dim confines of the tunnel, but if he had a chance to succeed at survival, he would have to take it.

But what about Protein and Click? Where were they being held? Fisher couldn't just leave them here with the prairie dogs, could he?

He knew what Click would say: Yes, leave Protein behind. Leave me behind. Your own survival is your only priority.

The lead prairie dog opened the bars.

"Come with me, human. Zapper is saving your life."

This time there was no bag over his head or rope around his wrists, but the prairie dogs kept their weapons ready and activated as they walked him through the tunnels. The underground complex snaked and twisted for what seemed like miles. Spacious chambers lining the tunnels were filled with neat bundles of leaves, bark, grasses, berries, snails, jars of bugs. Others contained workshops, with prairie dogs working leather, maintaining weapons, and taking apart blasted gadgets. Some sang as they worked, or chattered among themselves. And there were also little ones, prairie dog children, chasing each other and wrestling.

Despite the circumstances, the sights and sounds of the prairie dogs together in their colony made Fisher glad. He could only imagine how it must feel to be part of a community. He pictured himself bringing a netful of fish to a village, where perhaps a Forge made repairs to everyone's tools, and a Farmer tended neat gardens, and a Healer soothed Fisher's scrapes and cuts, and they'd all gather around blazing fires to eat together, maybe even sing.

He wished Click was with him. The robot would be trying to explain everything Fisher saw. He'd be talking about how the bare glass globes casting light through the tunnels drew their energy. And about prairie dog diets and the way societies organized themselves. And he'd help Fisher decide if the prairie dogs were his enemies because they'd attacked him, or friends because the gadgets were their common foes.

They arrived in a modest chamber furnished with a rough wooden table supporting a bowl of what looked like weeds. A weapon with a weathered blade hung on a wall peg. On a stool sat a pale-furred prairie dog, white scars criss-crossing her snout and belly. Fisher sensed great age, at least for a prairie dog. Her eyes nailed him with the keenest stare he'd ever experienced.

"Leave us, Red Top," she said to the leader of Fisher's escort party.

The guard captain sounded a brief growl. "Is not good idea, Mother. Human ape is dangerous."

She waved her paw, and after another moment's hesitation, Red Top retreated with his troop. But not before giving Fisher a dangerous glare. "We is right outside," he said.

Once he was gone, the old prairie dog bit down on some weeds from her bowl.

"You is hungry?" she asked.

"No." Fisher licked his dry lips.

"You is thirsty, maybe?"

"What have you done with my friends?"

"My name is Greycrown. Is colony's leader. Does human have a name?"

Fisher kept his mouth shut. He wouldn't say another word until he knew that Click and Protein were safe.

"Creatures that speak should have names," Greycrown said.

Fisher just stared at her until she barked something that sounded like a chuckle. "Mammoth is hokay," she said. "Is upground and is given food and water. Is unhappy and unruly, but unharmed. Machine is needing some new wires and parts, but dogs is good at fixing. Now you is telling Greycrown your name."

Fisher said nothing. Greycrown regarded him for a long time. *Munch, munch, munch.*

"Zapper is great traveler," she said into the silence. "Greycrown is sending her and Nailer to see where rovers come from. But she is saying you travel even farther."

No reason to lie about it. "Yes. From the other side of the continent. Me, Click, and Protein, all together. We're like . . ." Fisher grasped for words that would make the prairie dog leader understand. "We're like littermates."

Greycrown munched weeds.

"But they're not like me. Nobody else is like me. I'm the last living human from my Ark. There are more humans in the Southern Ark, but they aren't alive. Zapper told me about the Western Ark, though. She said it hasn't been destroyed yet, that the humans there are still alive. That's why I came all this way. To find them. To protect them against the gadgets. And to wake them up." He felt his heart quickening in his throat as he spoke. He was so close. He just needed a little more help.

Greycrown finished chewing and rose from her stool with a grunt. Fisher watched her pace around the little room. She turned to face him, her paws clasped behind her back.

"Ark is forbidden place. Is dangerous place. Is ringed with guns and death. Is—"

"Defense systems," said Fisher. "My Ark had them too. They became the gadgets, or what you call rovers. And at the Southern Ark, the defense systems became the Intelligence. But your people are tough and well armed. Together, I'm sure we could get past them. There'll be all sorts of advanced technology inside for you to scavenge—"

"Don't interrupt, human. Greycrown knows what is in Ark. Is specimens of all kinds, suspended in sleep. Is fish and foxes and cattle and older, stupider kind of prairie dogs. And, yes, is humans."

She said *humans* with such spite that it felt like a slap.

"Zapper told me humans made you," said Fisher. "They—we—cloned regular prairie dogs, and changed them. Weaponized them. You're smart because of us."

Greycrown munched weeds. "Hah. And you is thinking prairie dogs should be grateful to you? In awe of you? We is maybe thinking you is a god? We is singing songs to you?"

Well, that *would* have been awfully convenient . . .

"We is different than you, ragged human. Prairie dogs is remembering their own stories. Where we is coming from. How we remained while humans extincted. You humans dig more than you can ever put back. You burn anything that is burnable. You is destroying forests, is covering world with concrete and plastic, is changing weather. We is not impressed with you. Even if prairie dogs could get inside Ark, Greycrown is giving only one order: take it apart."

Fisher opened his mouth to protest, to tell her that's not what humans would do if he awoke them. But he'd seen their ruins. He'd depended on the junk they left behind. And he'd seen the destructive results of their technology. The gadgets. The Intelligence. The shopping mall above his head.

"If you're not going to help me, then at least let me and my friends go."

Greycrown took a handful of weeds. "Greycrown is not 'letting you go,'" she said. "Greycrown is kicking you out."

CHAPTER 21

Fisher expected Greycrown to order him tossed outside the dome, naked and alone with no food or water or supplies. So he was surprised when the captain of the guard presented him with a tube of hammered metal connected to a Y-shaped shoulder brace.

"Is blaster ball launcher," Red Top said. "See trigger there? Pull it, blaster balls fly, big boom. Here is pouch of blaster balls. Here is water bag. And here is pouch of food."

Fisher opened the food pouch.

"Dried fish?"

The captain grunted. "Zapper is saying you like."

"Where is Zapper?"

The captain snarled, as if the question made him angry, and he didn't answer. All he said was, "Follow. Is one more thing to give you."

Strange prairie dog vocalizations echoed through the tunnels as the captain led Fisher to the passage back up to the shopping mall, a whining yip-yip that sounded like pain.

"What's all that noise they're making?"

"Is the Cry of Leaving," said the captain. "Is song for the dead. Is for Nailer."

Nailer. That was the littermate Zapper had mentioned, the one who'd died trying to escape the gadgets with her.

Fisher didn't understand the point of making noise for the dead. If he made noise for every dead human—all those destroyed in his Ark, the ones killed by the Intelligence in the Southern Ark, the Stragglers—he'd never stop yipping.

From behind Fisher came a whirring sound. Then a click. "Ah, Fisher, here you are. I see you are ready to depart."

There stood Click. Or parts of Click. His head was patched with a plate of shiny metal. In place of his missing eye was a big, round multi-faceted lens. An entirely new chest plate was bolted onto his front.

"Click—are you . . . *you*?"

"The prairie dogs' weapon was designed to disable gadgets, not destroy them. That way, they are able to use their spare parts for new weapons of their own and other useful machinery. They say they have repaired the damage done to me."

"Robot is easy to fix," said Catches-Big-Bugs, who came down the corridor chewing a moth. "Is just wheels and rods. Is having to hammer some pieces to make fit, but now machine is stronger than before. Better. Faster. We is making him a good machine man."

"All very nice," said Red Top. "Now is time to go."

"What about Protein?"

"Yes, yes, is taking human and robot to big dung-dropper. Come."

Leaving behind the mournful Cry of Leaving, they climbed up another tunnel and emerged in the shopping mall. There, another patrol of prairie dogs kept their distance as Protein worked at reducing the size of a big mound of grasses and tree roots. He looked fine. The mammoth stopped eating and came over to Click. He offered Click a root, and Click clicked, a very comforting sound to Fisher.

"Hokay, hokay, you leave now," said the captain impatiently. With Click and Protein, Fisher followed the armed prairie dogs out of the mall, to the edge of the dome.

Zapper was waiting there, her zap stick on her shoulder. Fisher hadn't expected to see her again.

"I thought you were in the colony, doing the Cry of Leaving thing."

"Is already cried," she said. "Robot human is all fixed up?"

The captain grunted a yes.

"I am in superior working order," Click assured her.

"Is finding any . . . strange things . . . inside?"

Fisher had been wondering about that himself, but he didn't say anything.

The captain gave Fisher and Click a skeptical squint. "Mechanics say is finding sand and dirt and rocks and junk. Is something else?"

"No," Zapper said. "Zapper is hokay with what mechanics is finding."

Red Top opened the door in the dome and Fisher hurried ahead to be the first one out. The sun was sinking in the west, and a cold wind blew across the plain.

Click came out just behind Fisher. And following him came Zapper.

"What are you doing?" asked Fisher, confused.

"Zapper is traveling far, is seeing world that colony is hiding from. Is a world of cowering beasts, staying in the dark as rovers hunt them down, species by species. Human apes died because is refusing to change." Her sharp gaze focused on Red Top. "How is prairie dogs any different? Is entire world locked up in Ark, and we is too scared to look? Is a big dumb. You is telling Greycrown what Zapper says."

The captain gave Zapper a cold nod.

"Besides," Zapper said to Fisher, "we is sharing frog. Zapper goes with you."

Something told him to put a hand on Zapper's shoulder. "Thank you."

Red Top bared his teeth and stepped so close to Zapper that Fisher was afraid he'd bite her. "You is trying to find Ark for human?"

"Ai," said Zapper.

"Is mistake, sister."

"Is my mistake to make, Red Top."

Red Top turned now to Fisher. "Is mistake that brings death and destruction not just to humans, but to all. That is the way of human mistakes."

By their postures, Fisher thought the prairie dogs would fight. Instead they gently rubbed their muzzles together. Then, abruptly, Zapper turned away from her captain and led the companions away from the domed city.

CHAPTER 22

Zapper led them through the night, taking them into a maze-like network of canyons, where the walls grew so high the sky appeared as nothing more than a dark seam above their heads.

"My geography program has an entry for the Grand Canyon," Click said, his feet crunching over sand. "Is this it?"

Zapper shook her head. "Nai. Is old sewer system. Roof caved in many, many years ago. Earth fills it, water washes away, again and again and again. Is tricky land."

"You are navigating it with great confidence," said Click. "You have been here before?"

"Nai," said Zapper. "But elder dogs is coming here in earlier days." From her belt pouch, Zapper took a worn square of soft brown leather. She unfolded it to reveal a map. Little black paw prints marked prairie dog colonies. A convoluted line was the sewer-canyon. And at the end of the canyon was drawn a prairie dog skull. Zapper touched it with one of her claws. "Is where we go now," she said. "The Ark."

"You're risking a lot to take us there," Fisher said.

A confusion of things tugged his insides in different directions. He remembered when Click stepped between him and the rat, so many months ago. And when Fisher himself had run into the clearing to save Protein from the parrots. He still didn't understand what that was all about, why one person or animal or machine should risk its own life for the benefit of another. If survival was every living thing's goal, then shouldn't instinct or imprinting or programming prevent one from taking that kind of risk?

"Why are you doing this?" Fisher asked.

"Is bigger things than Zapper," said the prairie dog.

Plodding alongside Click, Protein came to a halt. The mammoth growled and shivered. Fisher knew what that meant. He held up a hand, and his companions stood still and quiet until the now-familiar whine of a gadget engine drew their gazes skyward.

A squadron of gadgets screamed overhead.

Without a word, Zapper surged ahead in a mad scamper. Rushing to keep up, Fisher fumbled to load blaster balls in his ball launcher. He'd counted eight gadgets flying over. If they destroyed the Ark before he even got there . . . No, there was no point in thinking that far ahead. Just focus on hurrying and getting ready to fight.

The canyon broadened into a round boulder field a few hundred yards across, ringed by high cliff walls.

"Is here!" Zapper shouted.

The gadgets hovered before a huge steel door set into one of the walls, their under-rotors kicking up clouds of dust. Truck-sized guns mounted above the door—the Western Ark's defense system?—aimed at nothing in particular.

A long silent moment hung in the air like smoke, and then the gadgets opened fire. The staccato hammering of their guns echoed off the walls, and soon a bitter stench of gun chemicals stung Fisher's nose.

He allowed himself one tiny breath of relief. If this was the Ark, he'd gotten here before the gadgets destroyed it. But just barely.

Click touched Fisher's shoulder to get his attention. "Fisher, this is the worst possible place for you. If the gadgets and the Western Ark's defenses engage in battle, you will become vulnerable to—"

The rest of Click's warning was cut off by the shriek of the gadgets launching their missiles. The projectiles struck the door and exploded, sending dirt and rocks tumbling to the valley floor. Smoke and dust cleared to reveal the door, now scarred and dented.

A low hum from somewhere rumbled, like a great engine, and the Ark guns swiveled on their turrets. They coughed into life, and the valley floor shook with artillery fire.

"Take out those gadgets!" Fisher called. He ran for the cover of a potato-shaped boulder, Protein and Zapper and Click right behind him.

Fisher took aim at a flying striker. His blaster ball would have struck a bulls-eye, but the gadget separated into a dozen smaller gadgets. Well, okay, Fisher thought. Big things, small things, it didn't matter to him, as long as he could make them dead things.

Something whizzed by his head, nearly scraping his temple. Fisher twisted around and fired. He laughed in satisfaction when his blaster ball struck the minigadget and it exploded in a puff of shrapnel and flame.

"Is how we kill them!" shouted Zapper, batting a minigadget out of the air with her zap stick. "With gnashing teeth and anger! Ai!"

A piercing whistle tore through the air, and on instinct, Fisher flattened himself, face in the dirt. There was a chest-thumping boom, and shattered rock rained down on him.

"That wasn't gadget fire," Fisher screamed, coughing. "That was from the Ark's guns."

The guns thundered away, their blasts coming as close to Fisher and his companions as to the gadgets.

"It does stand to reason," Click agreed. "The Ark defenses are treating everything before them as a threat. Including us."

"So it thinks I'm like a Straggler?"

"Perhaps," said Click, barely audible above the bursts and clatter of weapons fire. "Or perhaps it never expected a human to show up in the company of a custodial robot, a cloned pygmy mammoth, and a weaponized prairie dog."

Humans sometimes built the most cleverly idiotic machines, thought Fisher.

A whizzing sound came from his left. He turned just in time to see a dart, no bigger than a hummingbird, zeroing in on him. He fired, missed, fired again, and this time hit it.

He glanced around to see Zapper reduce a gadget to charred bits. Meanwhile, the Ark's guns pounded away.

A second wave of gadgets came over the canyon wall. There was a whole mob of them: spinning turtle machines, all-terrain gadgets on treads, machines that looked like knives on wheels. They moved like a fish school in a mass toward the Ark door. All the Ark guns turned on them, but even though they delivered heavier firepower, they were slower than the gadgets and hit few of their targets.

Fisher left the shelter of his boulder and ran after the gadgets, zigzagging his way from rock to rock and firing blaster balls. Sleeker and faster, Zapper raced ahead of him. Fisher heard Click sprinting, urging him to stay hidden, to stay safe.

"Stay with Protein," Fisher called over his shoulder, but the robot continued after him, and Protein pounded after Click. "Stop following me!" Fisher shouted, but it was no use. Click was determined to obey his programming, and he caught up to Fisher. They hid behind a rock just barely large enough to conceal Protein.

"What is your physical state, Fisher?"

"Annoyed!"

"Ah, you are confusing the emotional with the physical. Not to say that there isn't a close connection between the state of one's physical health and—"

"I'm fine," Fisher spat, shoving the robot down as a gadget missile streaked overhead. Protein laid his protective trunk over Click's back.

It was no use. His friends would not leave him.

"Just stay close to me, okay?"

"Well, yes," Click said. "That was always my intention."

Through all the explosions and fireballs and smoke clouds, Fisher caught another glimpse of the Ark door. It remained standing, but cracks were forming in the steel. It couldn't last forever. It might not last another five minutes.

A dome-shaped gunbot gadget rolled by with Zapper riding on top. Digging in with her claws to stay on, she used her one free paw to strike it with her zap stick, but the gunbot must have been well shielded, for the stick had no effect. Changing tactics, Zapper went to work with some screwdriver-like tool.

"We have to get between the gadgets and the door!" Fisher shouted after her.

"Just a few more connectors!" Zapper shouted back, and she leaped away as the gunbot rattled into disconnected pieces.

A chorus of yipping barks pierced the air, and with it

came prairie dogs, rappelling down the canyon. Led by Red Top, the war party carried zap sticks and guns. They carried lances and hand-held catapults and grenade launchers. They carried knives and throwing darts and ammunition. In a furious surge, they rushed into the canyon with fierce cries. All around, prairie dogs darted out from behind rocks and smoking machine carcasses to take shots at gadgets. Missiles and bullets whizzed overhead.

Zapper let out a vicious flurry of barks that sounded like celebration. She dove deep into the fray, Fisher firing blaster balls beside her.

The prairie dogs were skilled fighters, but it soon became clear the gadgets had them outnumbered and outgunned. For every shot a prairie dog got off, the gadgets drove them back to defensive positions with strafing runs and bombardments. And when it wasn't the gadgets pushing them back, it was the Ark guns.

Through bursts of flame and smoke balls, a reddish-brown streak dodged and dove across the field, finally reaching Fisher and his friends. It was Red Top. An ugly red gash marked his shoulder, fringed by crispy black fur. His wound did nothing to lessen his ferocious glare.

"You're helping us?" Fisher asked, astonished.

"No. Is coming to take back map Zapper stole from Greycrown. Is coming to bring her back and punish her."

Zapper clucked a bark that sounded like laughter. "If we

is not killed first by rovers, Zapper is going back with you. But first?"

Red Top showed his teeth. "Ai, ai. First, we is helping you. Is plan yet?"

"Yes," said Fisher, surprising everyone. "The plan is, you help me get inside the Ark."

Now it was Red Top's turn to cluck a bark that couldn't be anything but laughter. "Human is crazy, sister," he said to Zapper, not even bothering to look at Fisher. "Red Top is thinking best plan is to let rovers have human, and while they is taking him apart, we is making our retreat."

"Hear me out," said Fisher. "There's no way we can beat the gadgets, and no way they'll let us out of here alive. And even if they did, then it'd be the Ark guns' turn."

As if to illustrate Fisher's point, a gadget missile struck the rock they were standing behind, sending a spray of pebbles and grit into their faces. Fisher and the two prairie dogs ignored their stinging flesh and took aim at the offending gadget. Together, they blew it out of the air.

"Like I was saying," Fisher continued. "We can take cover inside the Ark. Maybe Click can take control of the Ark guns."

Fisher couldn't read Red Top's expression. It was too prairie dog.

"Human is right, brother," Zapper said, pausing to fire at a striker. "Is smart tactics."

Fisher was only going to give Red Top three seconds to

make a decision before breaking off for the door on his own.

"Prairie dogs is not retreating," Red Top said. "And Red Top is never leading his dogs into forbidden place. Nai, we is finishing these rovers, once and for all. But getting you inside Ark so you can use big guns . . . Ai, is making sense."

Red Top let out a series of yips. Other prairie dogs took it up and repeated it, and with great efficiency, a plan went into effect. Fighters converged on Fisher and his companions and formed a circle around them. As a group, they all ran for the Ark door, Click rattling and Protein trumpeting. Gadgets honed in on the group, concentrating their fire, but other prairie dogs shot at them from outside the circle. The Ark guns, taking advantage of the clustered gadgets, took out more of them.

The prairie dogs ganged up on the most lethal gadgets, blowing them up on the ground, shooting them out of the sky. Catches-Big-Bugs, armed only with a steel-tipped lance, jammed his weapon between the treads of a rolling metal monster with scorpion claws. The treads came loose and the gadget ground to a halt. The big prairie dog ripped open a panel and chewed circuitry until the gadget was dead.

The canyon was now littered with broken gadgets. Many of the remaining ones were out of ammunition, their guns uselessly clacking. There were still enough to pose a great threat, but maybe Fisher *could* save the Ark. Maybe without any prairie dogs losing their lives.

They'd almost reached the door when Fisher heard a sharp squeal just to his right.

"Zapper!"

She was down, clutching her leg with both forepaws. Blood streamed between her fingers.

Fisher rushed over to help her, but Zapper waved him away. "No, keep going," she gasped. "Finish your mission."

"I will," said Fisher, hoisting her over his shoulder. "But first I'm getting you to safety."

The Ark door was set back several feet into the cliff wall. Fisher found a nook in the rock and carefully lowered Zapper. Red Top got out a medical kit and began examining her wound.

She shivered. "Leave me here. Zapper is defending this position."

Fisher shook his head. "No, I'll find a way inside the Ark. You'll be safer there. All of you."

But leaning on her weapon, Zapper forced herself to her feet. Her legs shook, and her face expressed her pain. But she wouldn't relent. "We each has job to do. Fisher is protecting Ark from inside, Zapper is with her colony, protecting from outside. Now, go, before you is killed and all is for no purpose."

"Stay with her," Fisher said to Red Top.

The prairie dog captain nodded once, spread his legs, and with bristling fur, stood before Zapper. Fisher couldn't imagine anything getting past him.

Reluctantly, he turned his back. The door loomed before him, cratered and scorched, but still standing.

"How do we get in?"

"I do not know," said Click. "This Ark's entrance is as different from ours as the Southern Ark's was."

Looking closely, Fisher noticed an unmarked panel to the side of the door, shaped like a hand.

He knew what to do.

He spread his fingers and placed his palm flat against the panel. There was the barest hum as light from the panel outlined his fingers. Then, a sharp poke. Startled, Fisher pulled his hand away. Pin drops of blood beaded on each of his fingertips.

"Ah," said Click. "I believe your DNA has just been sampled. The builders of this Ark must have designed it assuming that someday an Ark-preserved human from somewhere else would find this place. It makes sense that they would give you the ability to make contact."

With a whisper, the massive door slid aside. Fisher could make out a dimly lit corridor ahead.

He gave one last look at Zapper and Red Top and Catches-Big-Bugs and the other prairie dogs. Gadgets formed up in the sun-bright sky, gathering for a final assault. The prairie dogs stood, snarling and yipping and barking. The captain hefted a shoulder catapult.

Guns thundering, the gadgets came at them.

"For the last time," Zapper barked, "*go!*"

Fisher and Click and Protein stepped into the Ark.

The door slid shut behind them.

CHAPTER 23

The din of battle faded to distant thunder once the door shut. A single strip of light overhead cast the corridor in a weak glow. The air felt untouched by warmth. Fisher and Click and Protein rushed down the corridor, until they came to a closed door with another hand-shaped panel beside it. The blood on Fisher's fingertips hadn't dried yet, and he hoped the building wouldn't demand a fresh supply any time he went through a door. Who knew how many doors there were?

"The building appears to be in good functioning order," Click said. "It should now have your DNA imprinted in memory and should not require more blood."

Fisher liked hearing things were working, but he didn't dare hope too much. Finding more dead humans would be a disappointment he'd never recover from.

He placed his hand in the indentation and the door opened with a *whoosh* onto a semicircular room. A set of control panels lined the wall, and screens and monitors hung above them, all dark.

"Can we control the guns from here?" Fisher asked.

Click fiddled with controls, waving away Protein's trunk.

"I believe I can turn the guns off, but I see no way to actually control them."

"Do it," Fisher said. "That'll at least give the prairie dogs an even chance against the gadgets."

Click touched some controls, and the panels came to life, with monitors and meters displaying data for temperature, chemical balance, and dozens of other factors. With a hum, shutters over the windows raised, revealing a cavernously vast, bowl-shaped chamber below. Fisher could see hundreds of pod beds. Or thousands. Blue light glowed through thick, bubbling gel. Behind the uncracked, clear lids of the pod beds lay the forms of animals. Fisher made out sheep and pigs and cows. There were musk ox and donkeys and llamas and tapirs. Gnus and kudu and beavers and skunks. The Ark teemed with specimens, more than Fisher had ever imagined in his visions of what the world before the Arks must have been like. Enough life to make him dizzy, like millions of stars spinning in a moonless black sky.

"Ah, yes, I have managed to deactivate the guns," said Click.

"The specimens," Fisher said. "Are they alive?"

After an agonizingly long time, Click said, "Ah. Yes.

Good. The specimens are all in good shape. They have not been tampered with."

"Should we wake them?" Fisher was anxious to see the humans awake and moving. He wanted to hear them speak. He wanted them to be people, not specimens inside boxes.

He didn't hear Click's response. His left ear flared with fire-hot pain, and he fell to his knees. It felt like his brain was trying to escape his head, and it hurt so bad he wished it would.

Click was there, leaning close and warbling on about something—probably asking Fisher what was wrong.

Fisher wanted to tell his friends that, if he died, they should wake the Ark, that the people might know how to protect themselves and defeat the gadgets.

And then, like an unraveling knot, the pain went away. All that was left was a tickling sensation traveling down his ear canal. A gleaming black worm wriggled on the floor before Fisher's eyes.

A nano-worm. One must have gotten inside him when he'd blown up the Intelligence. It had been living in his head ever since, like a parasite, using Fisher as transportation. He'd brought a piece of the Intelligence to the very last place he wanted it: the Western Ark.

Fisher tried to smack the worm with his palm, but still dizzy, he missed.

Trumpeting, Protein stamped toward it, but the worm scooted away and began crawling up Click's foot.

Finally, the robot noticed. He reached down, but the worm corkscrewed right into Click's metallic ankle, leaving behind a tiny hole.

Click whirred, not in his usual way. This noise was too loud, urgent, as if the robot would come apart.

"Click . . . ?"

"I believe . . . I am concerned that . . . ah, yes. The Intelligence is inside of me. We are struggling for control of my primary motivators."

The robot turned to the control panel and began touching switches.

"Ah, this is very bad," he said. "I appear to be shutting down life support systems. I am attempting to resist, but it wants to shut down the humans, and then inject itself into their flesh. Yes. Yes. This is bad. Please try to stop me, Fisher."

Fisher scrambled to his feet and grabbed Click's arm with both hands. The robot smashed a fist into Fisher's jaw. Fisher staggered back and looked at his friend in shock.

The numbers on the monitors were changing rapidly. Green lights turned to yellow.

"Fisher, your survival is at stake, and that of all the Ark specimens. You must destroy me."

Fisher lunged for the robot. He dodged Click's elbow once, but a second strike caught him in the nose. Blood spilled down Fisher's face. The prairie dogs' repairs had made Click fast and strong.

Protein snorted and stamped, his belly rumbling with a deep growl.

"I... cannot stop it. I am rerouting as many functions as I can... I cannot stop it." Click's fingers continued to dance over the controls. "It wants the humans. I am rerouting. You must destroy me, Fisher. I insist. Before it is too late. Use your blaster ball launcher. There is no other way."

"I'm not going to blow you up!" said Fisher. He came at Click again, but Click effortlessly shoved him back. On the monitors, yellow lights went orange, then red, and from red to black. Through the windows, Fisher saw pod beds below grow dark.

"I just prevented it from killing forty of the humans. But we lost the Bactrian camels," Click said. "Shoot me now, before there is nothing left alive."

"Click, I can't..."

"You must. I have now shut off life support systems for the Arabian camels as well. They are extinct."

Fisher raised his blaster ball launcher like a club and aimed a mighty swing at Click's head. The robot nimbly ducked, spun, and grabbed Fisher.

"I do wish you had listened to me," he said, as he lifted Fisher over his head and hurled him through the window.

Fisher plummeted amid a rain of glass.

CHAPTER 24

He landed atop a dark pod bed. Inside lay a juvenile Bactrian camel. Every dark pod bed meant a dead animal, and if all the animals of a kind died, its species would be extinct. Not because it was a weak animal, or because the kind of food it ate stopped growing, or because the world changed and the species didn't adapt to keep up. No. This was the doing of the twisted machine occupying Click's body. And humans had built the machine.

Groaning with pain and dread, Fisher slid feet-first to the floor and retrieved his blaster ball launcher.

Click's head appeared through the shattered window of the control room above.

"Do not come back up here," the robot called down. "If the Intelligence is given another chance, it will make me kill you. I am attempting to foil it by rerouting my motor systems, but you must use the manual controls on the pod beds to awaken as many specimens as you can before I shut them off. Quickly, Fisher. The Intelligence is making me kill the donkeys."

"Where are the humans?" Fisher shouted up.

"Three levels down. Hurry."

Fisher took a dragging step. His left ankle throbbed and wobbled when he put his weight on it. The fall had hurt him. He wiped blood from his forehead and limped over to a set of descending steps. Downstairs, row after row of pod beds contained humans, curled in their gel, with umbilical cords connected to their bare bellies. They looked so defenseless. Until now the only humans Fisher had ever seen were corpses. The skeletons of Stragglers, the un-alive Southern Ark humans, and the crushed humans back in his own Ark.

He brushed his fingers over the lid of a pod bed with a girl inside. The bubbles rising in the gel waved her hair.

A set of controls was inset at the foot of her bed. Click hadn't given him instructions, but it didn't look complicated: there were some meters, and a single, green button so big that it practically begged to be pushed.

So Fisher pushed it.

"Initiating awakening sequence on pod HS4B, adolescent human female," said a soothing voice from the bed. "Does operator wish to disconnect umbilical?"

Operator?

Oh. The pod meant him.

"Click!" he shouted up to the control room. But Click didn't answer. The only sounds from above were Protein's agitated snorts and growls. Then, a distinctly angry squeal from the mammoth, followed by a clang of metal and a plasticky crunch of impact, and Click came sailing through the window. He landed in a crumpled heap on the floor, a few pod beds away from Fisher. His arms and legs were folded beneath his torso, which had a tusk-sized hole gouged into its side. But it was the robot's head that had taken the full impact of the fall. It was bent so far behind him that the back of Click's skull was resting between his shoulder blades.

"The Intelligence is running a damage assessment on me, Fisher. Motor systems are suboptimal but functional. Balance and navigation units are suboptimal but functional."

Click's legs straightened. He slowly unbent one of his arms.

"Fisher, load your weapon with all the ammunition you have and destroy me."

"You mean kill you," screamed Fisher. "I'm not going to let the Intelligence force me to do that."

Click unbent his other arm. His fingertips scraped the smooth, glossy floor. "You must listen to me. You have risked your own death numerous times. You have ended the lives of fish and small animals and used their resources to continue your own existence. Death is a necessary component of survival, Fisher. You know this. Kill me, before the Intelligence makes me kill you."

Yes, Fisher had killed and hunted. But this was different. Click was a friend. If he could kill Click to survive, that meant he could kill anything, use anything, destroy anything. And that wasn't survival. That was just doing what his ancestors had done.

"There has to be another way," he said. "Help me figure it out."

With a metallic groan, Click's head rose. His multifaceted eye glowed blue in the reflected light of the pod beds.

"I am coming for you, Fisher. Please run."

Fisher lurched away, fast as he could along the curving walkway. He tried to ignore the searing pain in his ankle as Click's footfalls gained on him. Stumbling more than running, he hurried down the steps to lower levels.

"You are escaping at insufficient speed, Fisher. I urge you to hide."

Fisher ducked down and slipped between two pod beds. He couldn't outrun Click, and he doubted he could hide from him for long.

"I need a way to disable you that won't destroy you," he called out. "Like the way the prairie dogs did back at the mall."

"They shot me with a shock claw," said Click, clanking after Fisher in pursuit.

"All I have is blaster balls!"

"I am aware of that. You must use them, Fisher."

But Fisher had seen what blaster balls could do to

gadgets. He knew they'd blow Click to scrap. He had to find another way to stop him. But how? Thanks to the prairie dogs, Click was lethally fast and strong. And Fisher's weapon was useless against him if he wasn't willing to use it.

"You must hide more quietly," Click said. "The Intelligence is using my auditory senses to locate you."

Back in the domed city the prairie dogs had used a shock claw to jolt and stun Click with electricity. It had damaged him, but not destroyed him.

Fisher had an idea. A terrible idea.

"Where are the aquatic creatures?" he called to Click.

"Four rows down, thirteen degrees to your left. Stop talking, please, Fisher. I can hear you."

Fisher staggered down more stairs and followed the curving wall to his left. He needed a fish with a strong-enough electric current. Eels would be great. Or electric catfish. Or . . . yes. Panting, he came to a stop before a cluster of pod beds. Inside floated a spotted, winged fish. A numbfish. If he awoke one, if he left its life-giving umbilical in place, if he placed it on the ground in a slick of gel and tricked Click into crossing its path . . .

Click stepped into the corridor.

"Drawing on your fishing imprint was very inspired, Fisher. I only wish you had thought of it sooner. You are too late. The Intelligence is willing to sacrifice you to gain unrestricted access to the rest of the humans. It will use my hands to crush your windpipe. Please flee, Fisher. I am running at you now."

And Fisher fled, down more stairs and between two rows of pod beds containing muscular breeds of dogs. These were work dogs, for shepherding livestock, for pulling sleds. Humans had bred animals for particular purposes, selecting traits they found useful or pleasing. The world had given them wolves, and humans had reshaped them into dogs. Humans had changed the world.

The Ark around him was Fisher's world, and he needed to find a way to use it to his advantage.

He bounced from pod bed to pod bed. Goats, sheep, pigs... None of these would do. With the sounds of Click approaching and his ankle screaming, he hurried down another level. And there he found what he was looking for.

Fisher slapped a green button.

"Initiating awakening sequence on pod UAH-D, adult *ursus arctos horribilis*, male. Does operator wish to disconnect umbilical?"

"Yes," Fisher snapped. "And hurry!"

The pod gel stopped bubbling and drained away.

Wet fur glistening, the mammal inside remained curled up and still. Then, with a moist pop, the umbilical came loose and retracted into the pod bed.

"*Ursus arctos horribilis*, male UAH-D is now self-sustaining. Does operator wish to initiate full brain function?"

"Yes!"

Fisher remembered how he'd felt when he first became born. He'd been confused, and scared, and hungry. His instinct told him to flee when faced with threats.

He hoped this animal's instinct would tell it something else.

"Fisher, you are making the most inefficient escape I have yet witnessed since your awakening." Click stood leaning over the rail, one level above him.

"I came up with a plan to stop you—"

"Do not tell me," Click said. "The Intelligence is conscious and will use anything you tell me to its advantage. Even now, it is attempting to overwrite my personality programming. I am finding myself motivated to strangle you. Hello."

Click leaped over the rail and dropped heavily before Fisher. Turning, Fisher sprinted several yards down the walkway, but the robot was too fast and caught him easily. He reached out, wrapping his white fingers around Fisher's throat. It felt like knives clogging Fisher's airway. He could get only the thinnest trickle of breath.

"Fight it," he rasped.

"I cannot," Click said, his voice calm as ever. "You must fight it. You must be the strongest animal. Your survival depends on it."

A curtain of gray fell over Fisher's vision, and everything felt so heavy.

Fisher's left hand scrabbled at Click's chest. In his right, he still held his blaster ball launcher. The robot squeezed Fisher's throat tighter and lifted him in the air. The tips of Fisher's toes scraped the floor.

"I wish you had heeded my advice and destroyed me," said Click. "Once the Intelligence is done making me kill you, it will turn its attention to killing the humans in the pods. Then it will infiltrate their flesh with copies of itself to preserve them. These tasks run counter to my programming. I must tell you, Fisher, I would rather be permanently deactivated than do these things."

Fisher raised his blaster ball launcher. He placed the end of the barrel against Click's chest.

"No," said Click. "Aim for my head. The nano-worm is lodged deep in my central behavioral processor. You must destroy my brain."

A throaty growl came from behind Click. *Ursus arctos horribilis.* The grizzly bear Fisher had awoken. Seven feet tall, the grizzly rose up on two legs, all thick brown fur and sharp claws and clean white fangs.

"I'm sorry, Click," Fisher choked. "I found a way."

Bears were excellent fishers. They possessed fantastic reflexes. They were strong and fast. And powerful enough to take on a robot.

"Ah, yes. Excellent, Fisher."

The bear dropped back down on all fours and charged, half a ton of wild fury focused on the only thing in its path.

Click turned his head just as the bear's paws slammed into his back.

Click struck the ground, and Fisher with him. Gripping his weapon, he crab-crawled away. The grating squeal of the bear's claws raking Click's body made Fisher wince. Plastic and metal cracked and crunched as the bear ripped Click apart. Hydraulic fluids sprayed as its jaws closed on one of Click's arms and tore it free.

"Fisher," came Click's voice, weak and full of static, "try to make the bear remove my head plate and get to my brain. The nano-worm will otherwise attempt to squirm free and infiltrate some other device . . ."

The bear's fangs sank into Click's head. Claws pried loose his temple, exposing wires and connectors and a black, fist-sized object shaped roughly like a closed clam shell. Click's brain.

"Ah, yes. Very good."

"I'm sorry, Click. I didn't want to . . . I'm sorry."

"You have done very well, Fisher. You used your fishing knowledge and controlled your environment. But I must urge you to be cautious. When the bear is done with me, it will turn on you."

Click's voice was barely a hissing whisper now. The bear ripped an eye free.

"I'm sorry," Fisher said, again and again, nearly blinded by his tears.

"Do not be. You are a successful animal, Fisher. You

survived. And not just for your own sake, but for the benefit of your entire species."

Snarling, the bear forced its paw into Click's head cavity. Its claws scratched at Click's brain.

"You succeeded, too, Click. You helped me survive. You helped all of us survive, to repopulate the Earth. Thank you."

"Ah, you are welcome. Now, I must remind you, do not forget to destroy the worm. It is very important that you destroy—"

"I will," Fisher said.

And Click's voice dropped into a soft, rhythmic clicking. The clicking grew slower and ever softer, until it fell away into permanent silence.

Fisher rose to his feet.

He aimed his weapon at the floor in front of the bear and fired. The *ka-poom* of his blaster ball echoed through the Ark and left a sizzling hole in the floor. The newly awoken grizzly moaned a roar, then turned and fled into the maze of the pod beds.

And there, wriggling away from the parts that used to be Click's head, was the black thread of a nano-worm, making its way toward an air vent in the wall.

Fisher loaded a blaster ball and curled his finger around the trigger.

He took aim.

He knew he would not miss.

CHAPTER 25

He could still hear the growling and snuffling of the grizzly in the darkness and so kept his blaster ball launcher ready as he made his way back to Protein in the control room.

Protein lowed and touched Fisher all over with his trunk.

"I'm okay," he said, patting Protein. "Just a little bit busted up. Stay here, okay? I'm going to go out and . . . Well, just stay here."

Fisher left the control room and started down the corridor to the Ark entrance. Protein, not at all to Fisher's surprise, ignored his request to remain back and followed, snorting.

Fisher dreaded opening the Ark door. He feared he'd find the canyon swarming with gadgets and littered with burning clumps of prairie dog fur. But when he stepped out into the searing bright sunlight, the smoking clumps on the battlefield were all machines. Prairie dogs poked through debris, organizing the wreckage into sorted piles of scavenge. The fight had become a salvage operation.

Red Top stood just outside the door, yipping and barking out orders. He barely acknowledged Fisher's return. But Zapper, leaning on a gadget rotor blade as a crutch, showed her teeth in an expression Fisher recognized as the closest thing prairie dogs had to a smile.

"Prairie dogs is victorious," she said with a yip. "Silver Paw and Swiftdig is injured, but is getting healed soon."

Fisher's chest untightened. "That's good. Prairie dogs is mighty."

"Ai, we is mighty. Is Ark all alive inside?"

"The specimens are intact," Fisher said, fighting against the cloud of sadness blanketing him. "Most of them, anyway."

Zapper grunted. "Where is robot?"

"Click . . . I failed him."

With reluctance, Fisher filled her in on what had happened inside the Ark, including the way he'd used the bear against Click. He did not feel proud of himself relating the story.

"Maybe mechanics can fix?" Zapper said.

"Not this time," Fisher said.

Zapper gently patted his hip, her whiskers drooping. Even Red Top seemed saddened by this news.

Fisher told the rest of the story, about the nano-worm he'd reduced to dust. And about the grizzly bear still on the loose. He emphasized its size and strength and teeth and claws. The captain's eyes went wide.

"We should . . . subdue beast," Red Top said, his eyes shifting uneasily.

"No," Fisher said. "I know it's a forbidden place for you. I'll do it."

"I do it with you," Zapper said, firmly. She barked across the boulder field. "Dullclaw, Shaper, Quicktail! Is salvage job for us in Ark!"

Red Top made a coughing noise. "Red Top helps too. Backstripe, Goodfoot! Not just be standing there, is bringing ropes and net!"

The work continued into the campfire-lit night. Fisher's wounds were cleaned and bandaged, and his injured ankle splinted, and he allowed himself to rest while the prairie dogs hauled gadget parts back to the colony.

But his rest was short-lived.

He went back inside the Ark and painstakingly gathered the parts of Click, including his fragile brain, which no amount of glue or wire or screws would be able to fix.

Zapper helped him place the pieces on a blanket, which Fisher folded and carried in a bundle back outside. The prairie dog warriors had built a fire. Creosote embers rose on the updrafts, blinking out well before reaching the stars.

The prairie dogs began howling with long cries that sounded both fierce and mournful. Fisher recognized the tones and patterns. It was the Cry of Leaving, the same one they'd sung for Zapper's fallen littermate, Nailer, and the ceremony was well underway before Fisher fully realized what was happening. It was a funeral, for Click.

He carefully set the bundle of Click's remains near the fire.

One by one, prairie dogs laid small offerings atop it. Catches-Big-Bugs put down a fat moth. Red Top contributed a broken lance. Other prairie dogs left bits of weapons, or small bundles of grasses, or prickly pear cactus fruit. Protein hauled over an absurdly large saguaro branch. He ran his trunk over the blanket filled with Click's parts and made a low sound through his trunk. Then he began eating the cactus fruit.

Zapper placed something in Fisher's hand. "Is not tradition for prairie dogs, but maybe for humans?"

In Fisher's palm was a small piece of glass-like substance, attached to a leather thong. A piece of Click's eye.

"I don't know what human traditions are," Fisher said. "I always thought Click would be here to tell me."

Zapper grunted. "Robot pretty smart, but smartest thing robot knew is that Fisher is very smart. You is inventive. You is figuring it out."

Fisher smiled, just a little, and looped the thong over his head. Surprisingly heavy, the piece of Click settled over his heart.

. . .

"Walk with me, human."

Greycrown had come out to see the Ark for herself. She did not look pleased.

Alone, Fisher gave her a tour. She lingered a long time before the pod beds housing sleeping prairie dogs. They were smaller than her kind, with much in common, but no more than Fisher shared with chimpanzees. She lingered even longer before the humans. They remained in stasis, including the girl whose birthing sequence Fisher had started.

"Is many dangerous things here," Greycrown said. "You is wanting to awaken everything, I am thinking?"

"Of course not. There's not a habitat for everything. There's not food for everything. I mean, some of the pod beds have hammerhead sharks in them. Click said the idea is to wake things gradually, over the course of many years, when there's a place for them. When the world is ready. In fact . . . I'm not sure I should be waking up *anything*."

"But is why you fought Intelligence and rovers. Is why you is journeying across grassland and desert and carnivorous jungle. Is why you come down river. Thousands of miles, and thousands of hardships. You is scared, now that there is just some buttons to press?"

"Yes," said Fisher. "I'm scared. Anyway, you said if you ever got inside the Ark, you'd give the order to destroy it."

"That is what Greycrown is saying to you in colony, yes."

Fisher directed the hardest look he could summon at

the prairie dog leader. "But you know I'm not going to let you do that."

She waved a dismissive paw at him. "Greycrown is not caring about you. But Zapper will not let Greycrown destroy Ark. Even Greycrown's own captain of troops will not let her. Colony chose to help human. Now is question: what will human choose?"

Fisher didn't have an answer for Greycrown yet. He walked away from her, down the corridor and back out into the open air.

When morning broke, he was once again inside the Ark.

For the last few hours, he'd been standing over the pod bed housing the girl whose awakening sequence he'd started yesterday. Physically, she was fine, but not conscious. With a few buttons and vocal commands, Fisher could return her to full and complete slumber.

"I thought everything would be easy if I found an intact Ark with living specimens," he said to Protein. "Just punch some buttons or throw some switches and wake everyone up. They'd know what to do, and I could let them take charge. I'd catch fish for them, and they'd rebuild civilization, and everything would take care of itself."

Protein snuffled.

"It's just . . . there's a lot to do."

Fisher's fingers brushed over the lid of the pod bed housing the girl.

What kind of human would she be?

What would she make of the world she awoke to?

What would she make of Fisher?

Protein ran his trunk over Fisher's head, and Fisher touched the glass hanging around his neck. Then, with a firm hand, he reached out for the big green button.

CHAPTER 26

She came awake in a bed of bubbling gel.

And this is what she knew:

Her name was Hunter.

The world was dangerous.

But she was not alone.

ACKNOWLEDGMENTS

Writing a book is a lot like taking a journey, and I had a great deal of help along the road. The following people provided guidance, advice, maps, fuel, way stations, snacks, and repairs, and it might have been a pretty crummy trip without them.

My thanks go first and foremost to my road buddy Lisa Will, for life support and defense systems.

Special thanks as well to my agent, Caitlin Blasdell, who navigates me through the often confusing roads of the book business, and to my editor, Margaret Miller, whose gentle but insistent feedback whenever I got tired or lost helped make this a much better book than it would otherwise be. Much appreciation goes to the entire team at Bloomsbury, whose care and expertise turned my manuscript into the book you now hold in your hands. And big thanks to August Hall for his beautiful, evocative cover art.

The Blue Heaven and Starry Heaven writers' workshops provided useful getaways with plenty of fun and camaraderie, and, most importantly, smart feedback on portions of this book at various stages, so thanks to Paolo Bacigalupi, Brad Beaulieu, Gwenda Bond, Tobias Buckell, Sarah Kelly Castle (who also came up with this book's title), Deb Coates, Brenda Cooper, Robert Levy, Sandra McDonald, Holly McDowell, Catherine Morrison, Heather Shaw, William Shunn, and Rob Ziegler. And for slogging through the entire manuscript, my gratitude to Kris Dikeman and Adam Rakunas.

Additional thanks to Rae Carson (who held a mirror up to my opening to show me the ending), C.C. Finlay (who drew me a map), Sarah Prineas (for answering my call for emergency roadside assistance), and Jenn Reese (whose ideas on everything from structure to funny character bits proved invaluable).

Thanks also to Mike Jasper, Karen Meisner, Tim Pratt, Jeremiah, Theo, and Maud.

Finally, my thanks to all the technology I relied on throughout the writing of this book, from my laptop to my smartphone to my coffeemaker. Truly, we live now in an age of wonders.

Greg van Eekhout

is the author of the middle-grade novel *Kid vs. Squid* and the adult fantasy *Norse Code*. He lives in San Diego, California.

www.writingandsnacks.com

Read on for a selection from Greg van Eekhout's

KID VS. SQUID

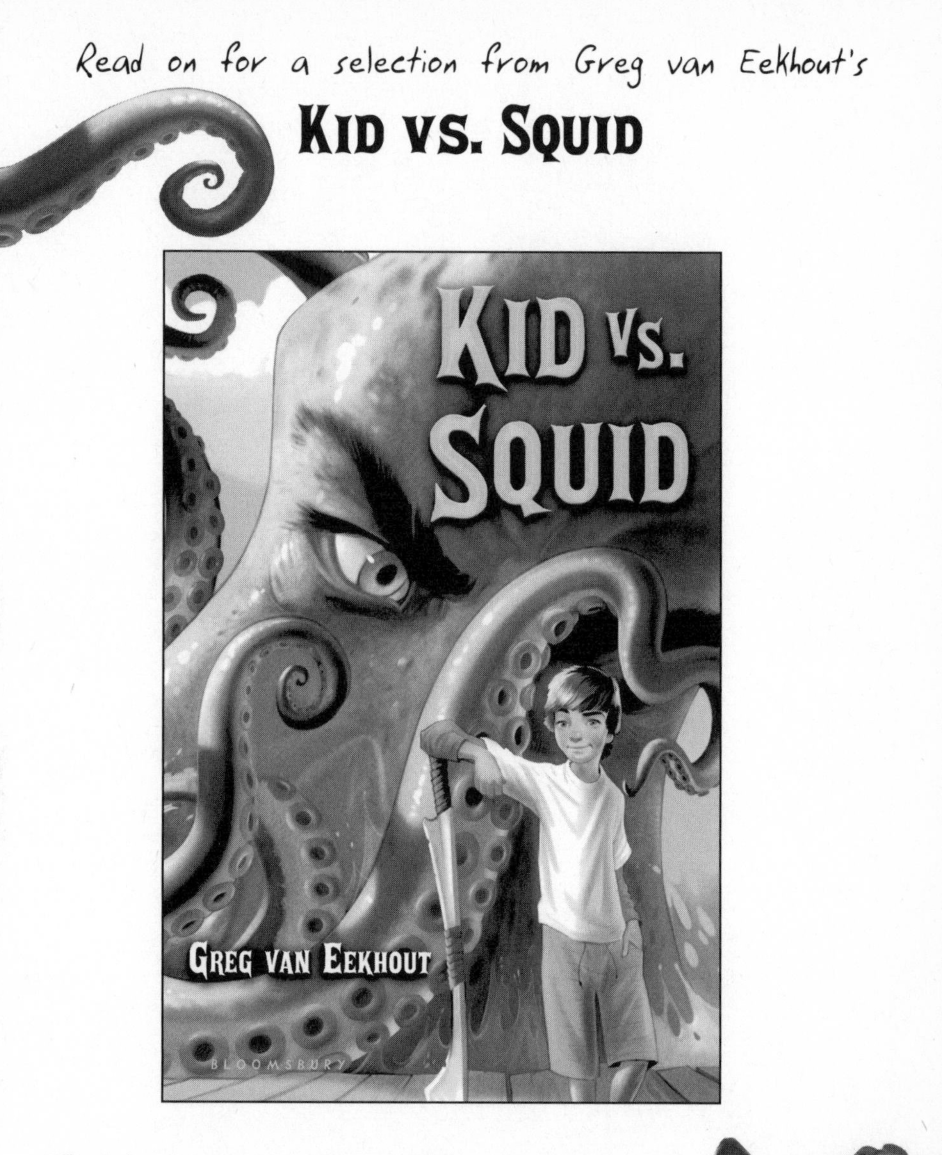

Thatcher's quiet summer job at his great-uncle's seaside museum becomes a wild adventure after a mysterious girl appears—she's from the lost city of Atlantis, and its people need Thatcher to save them.

Dear Thatcher,

I'm off conducting some very important museum business. Here's your to-do list. And remember, a ship can't set sail without wind, so make sure you eat something.

—Uncle Griswald

TO-DO LIST

1. Water the plants
2. Feed Sinbad
3. Dust the shrunken heads
4. Clean the What-Is-It?? (but don't open the box!!!)
5. Have some lunch (pizza in fridge)

So far I'd gotten as far as Number Two on Uncle Griswald's list. Sinbad the tabby was lapping up tuna-liver mix in my bedroom, which was really just a hammock in the closet where Griswald kept his mops and buckets. I tried not to mind so much. Believe me, there were worse places in the museum. For example, most of it. I couldn't even walk to the bathroom without passing a glass case containing four tiny severed heads with fins for ears. Dead-eyed, they grinned fiercely, daring me to touch them with my feather duster.

Me, Thatcher Hill, versus the shrunken heads. This was my summer vacation.

I was supposed to be spending the time between sixth and seventh grades traveling through Asia with my parents. They owned the biggest squirt gun distributorship in Arizona, and they were touring overseas squirt gun factories in exotic and interesting places. But one of my classmates had caught some kind of kangaroo rat virus, and even though I didn't get sick, I was exposed and wasn't allowed to travel out of the country. I'd begged my folks to let me stay with friends in Phoenix, but they decided I should be watched by family. My closest relative was Mom's uncle, my great-uncle Griswald, so they shipped me off to live with him in Los Huesos, California.

I'll have plenty more to say about Los Huesos later. Right now, I want to tell you about Uncle Griswald's museum.

Maybe you've been to a museum on a school field trip. Maybe there were dinosaurs or old paintings or statues of naked people inside. Griswald's museum wasn't like that. Professor Griswald's Museum of the Strange and Curious and Gift Emporium sat crammed on the Los Huesos boardwalk between a hot dog stand and a tattoo parlor. Here, Griswald displayed things that looked like they'd been dredged up from a deep ocean trench where all the ugliest sea creatures live because it's dark and nobody has to look at them there. He had a fish with a green handlebar mustache in a jar. He had a hand with suction cups and eyeballs. And a thing that looked half-fish and half-monkey, labeled the Feejee Mermaid. A tiny, withered man with pants made of sardines. An octopus with sneakers on the ends of its eight arms. The shrunken heads. And so forth.

He even kept a mummy in a glass-lidded sarcophagus, resting on a pair of sawhorses. It was the color of beef jerky, with dark black squiggles down its arms that looked like sea horses. Griswald said the squiggles were tattoos. I thought they were done in Magic Marker. The mummy had no head. Mummies *with* heads cost a lot. He'd found this one washed up on the beach, which was his favorite way to acquire exhibits, since it was free.

Places like my uncle's used to be called dime

museums, because marks (another word for "customers," or "suckers") were charged a dime to gawk. Uncle Griswald charged three dollars.

I gave the shrunken heads a quick pass with my feather duster and moved on to the *What-Is-It??*

So, what was it?

It was a barnacle-encrusted wooden box with swirly grain that reminded me of ocean waves. One side had a window of bubbly green glass, and through the glass, you could almost see a face looking back at you: pale eyelids, a sharp blade of a nose, and a wide, thin-lipped mouth turned down in a grimace. Griswald said it was a very important head, but he couldn't remember exactly what made it so important. He'd had an accident of some kind a while back, and it had messed him up in a lot of ways, his memory included.

I smacked the feathers of my duster against the box a few times and wiped the glass with a damp cloth. The museum was now as ready for visitors as it ever would be, but so far this morning, nobody had walked past the door, much less come inside.

According to the to-do list, it was time for lunch. I went to the fridge in Uncle Griswald's cramped little kitchen and excavated a take-out pizza box from beneath two six-packs of beer. Normally the thought of cold pizza would fill me with a sense of joy and wonder, because if there's a more perfect food than pizza, it's *cold* pizza. But this pizza was made of evil. The cheese resembled the inside of an orange peel. The toppings looked like something left behind by seagulls.

I closed the box.

"Aren't you going to eat that?"

Leaning on a crutch, Griswald filled the kitchen doorway. He looked like a cartoon sailor, with a windburned red face fringed by a white beard. Taking in his black wool cap and matching sweater, I figured he'd probably been out throwing harpoons at whales. I still didn't know what had happened to his left leg, but half of it wasn't there.

"I'm not hungry this morning, I guess."

He gave me a look that I didn't know how to read. He'd never been married and wasn't used to having kids around, and I wasn't used to spending time with crusty old mariners.

"Well, all right," he said. "If you're not going to eat it—"

I thrust the pizza box at him, grateful when he took it from my hands.

"I'm done dusting the exhibits," I said. "I thought I'd take a walk out in the cold, damp air."

Griswald nodded thoughtfully, his jaw working on

balsa-wood pizza crust. "It's a fine day for it. But if you comb the beach, watch your step. Lots of wickedness on the shore this time of year."

"Wickedness? You mean like toxic syringes?"

He was about to answer my question, but then seemed to forget what he was going to say. "Just be careful."

I left the museum behind and headed down the boardwalk. Perched on the edge of a crumbling sandstone cliff above the beach, the boardwalk was a half-mile strip of weathered planks, possibly salvaged from a pirate ship. T-shirt shops and pizza stands and other touristy joints stretched out into the fog. Almost all of them were shuttered and closed. Even though it was the first week of June, the tourists still hadn't arrived.

I leaned over the guardrail and looked down across the beach. This was not a golden-sand, volleyball-net, bikini-girls kind of beach. This was more of a rocky, driftwood, kelpy kind of beach. Not a place where you'd slather yourself with sunblock and lay out on a towel with a paperback book. For one thing, the smell of rotting seaweed would detract from your enjoyment. Also, you'd have to share space with a lot of dead fish. Everything the ocean couldn't stomach washed up on this beach.

Los Huesos was Spanish for "the bones," and the

town was built on a huge slab of rock that jutted out to sea like a broken middle finger, flipping off the Pacific Ocean. Offshore, scattered boulders stood like the guano-glazed vertebrae of a giant.

I turned away from the rail to find I was being watched.

Two guys about my size sat on BMX bikes in front of the shut-down saltwater taffy stand. They wore hoodies with the hoods up, their faces hidden behind big sunglasses and bandannas.

"Hey," I said, raising my hand in a dorky little wave.

They didn't reply. They didn't move. Their gloved hands gripped the handlebars of their bikes. It was a cold day, but not worth bundling up for. Maybe they had some condition that made them sensitive to sunlight.

Wordlessly, they pedaled the few yards over to me until their knobby front tires almost touched my shins. My legs told me to run, but I wasn't going to listen to my wussy legs. I'd had six months of tae kwon do training when I was nine. I'd made it to green belt.

"You wanna back off a bit?" I said, trying to make it sound less like a request and more like a threat. Unfortunately, tough-guy talk had never been my biggest strength. I'm more jokey than punchy-kicky. Jokes are my armor.

Back in elementary school everyone knew me, and

I knew everyone, and they called me by my first name, and I called everyone by their first names. That was the natural way of things in elementary school. But there's nothing natural about middle school. Middle school is just a very unnatural place. It's too big, a landfill where all the kids graduating from nine elementary schools get dumped. Instead of a few hundred classmates, I have a couple thousand. In elementary school I was Thatcher. In middle school, I'm a last name.

Middle school made me funny-mean. My mouth started getting me in trouble. I respond to bullies and teachers with funny comments, sharp little put-downs, and sometimes if my victim shows signs of weakness, I can't stop myself. My words are like a cheetah taking down a gazelle by the throat.

These weird guys didn't seem like gazelles.

"Are you flotsam?" one of them said in a slushy voice. It sounded like he needed to swallow. Let's call him Left.

"Am I *what*sam?"

The other one, Right, pulled a small book from his pocket. The cover was made of two clam shells, joined by a hinge. "He can't be flotsam," Right gurgled. "He's not in the book."

"We've never seen you before, so you're not a townie," said Left.

"But since you're not in the book, you can't be flotsam," said Right.

"We're done here," Left said to his brother or friend or co-freak. "But we'll be watching you."

With that, they turned their handlebars, and when they did, the cuff of Left's sleeve rode up and I caught a brief glimpse of his wrist. The skin was white and shiny. A little bit transparent. I could see thin black veins branching below his flesh. I thought of an entire arm that looked like that, a face that looked like that, and I tried to stop thinking about it, because it was making me kind of sick to my stomach.

"I'll be watching you watching me," I said, this time with a *deliberately* dorky wave. The boys popped wheelies and rode off.

Later, back at the museum, Griswald and I were having dinner. And by dinner, I mean Wonder bread and some kind of cheese substance that sprayed from a can. Sitting at a folding card table, Griswald told me about his day, which mostly involved searching the thrift shop downtown for used sneakers. "For the octopus," he explained.

"What's wrong with the sneakers it's wearing?"

"Everybody deserves fresh sneakers," Griswald said, very seriously.

"And I suppose being a cephalopod who lives in a jar doesn't change that."

"Exactly," he said, wiping cheese substance from his mouth with a paper towel. "Did you have a good walk?"

"I did. I smelled a lot of kelp."

"Excellent. Did anything interesting happen?" He made it sound like a casual question, but I could tell there was something he *wasn't* asking, as if he was worried what my answer might be.

I thought about the weird guys on the bikes. And I thought about my great-uncle, sitting across the rickety table from me, whose biggest concern was buying shoes for a pickled octopus.

"No," I said. "Nothing interesting."

"Ah."

I couldn't tell if he was disappointed or relieved.

"May I have some more cheese spray, please?"

That night, curled up in my hammock as Sinbad nested in my suitcase, I dreamed of jellyfish. They stared down on me with almost-human eyes.

Mr. Cheeseman

and his three attractive, polite, relatively odor-free children are on the run. From what?

Well, that's a whole nother story. . . .

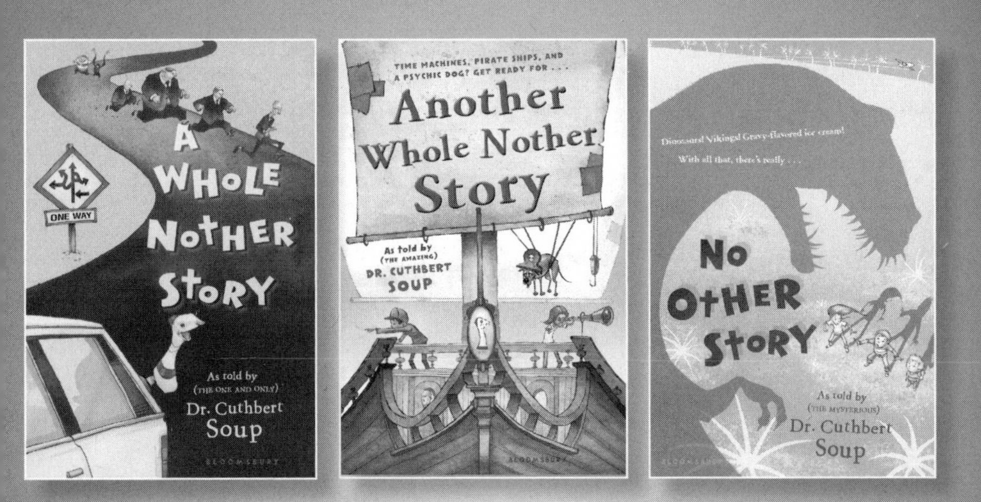

"If you take yourself very seriously, perhaps this isn't the book for you. But if you're in the mood for a lot of silliness and reading about a really interesting and quirky family, then it's perfect."

—Wired.com/GeekDad

www.awholenotherbook.com

www.bloomsburykids.com